Charlotte Haptie

Illustrated by Pete Williamson

Hodder Children's Books
A division of Hachette Children's Books
338 Euston Road, London NW1 3BH
An Hachette UK company
www.hachette.co.uk

For Ella Sills
– Charlotte Haptie

To Lynne
– Pete Williamson

1

Magic in the Shed

Delilah Smart lived with her parents, Granny Grabbers and Sir Isaac Newton, her brain-building alphabet bear. Her parents were always rushing around, exercising and going to work. It was Granny Grabbers – the extraordinary childcare robot – who loved her and looked after her.

Today was Saturday. Granny Grabbers was in the garden shed trying to learn how to do a magic trick. It was all about playing cards and sleeves. She was wearing a top hat and a special magician's jacket that she had made herself. It had six sleeves, one for each of her six grabbers, and lots of secret pockets.

Granny Grabbers had a round head, no visible neck and her body was barrel-shaped, with tiny wheels underneath. Just now she looked like a very large purple ball covered in stars. The magician's coat was much too big. The hat kept falling down over her headlamps.

Now she couldn't remember where she'd hidden the card. It could be up a sleeve. Or perhaps it was in a secret pocket.

Dr Doomy the gerbil watched her politely.

'This your card?' Granny Grabbers asked in her husky voice.

She stuck a grabber in a sleeve and produced an egg whisk. This had nothing to do with the magic trick and must have been left over from breakfast.

Dr Doomy put his head on one side. He was a very clever gerbil and he knew the difference between the king of hearts and a kitchen utensil.

At that moment Delilah opened the door of the shed.

'Child Unit, reverse!' commanded Granny Grabbers. 'Private magical practice!'

Delilah reversed.

'Is *this* your card?' Granny Grabbers asked Dr Doomy sternly.

He twitched his whiskers. She had pulled a squashed-looking lettuce from somewhere deep in one of her armpits.

'Can I come in now?' called Delilah.

'More practice to make perfects,' muttered Granny Grabbers, giving Dr Doomy some of the lettuce. She took off the top hat and the king of hearts fell out on to the floor. Then she started trying to take off the magician's jacket. She didn't usually wear clothes and certainly nothing with sleeves. Hats were OK . . . and gloves . . . and scarves . . . but this . . .

'Are you OK?' called Delilah anxiously. She could hear a lot of grumbling and beeping. Then scuffling, a crash and much ruder grumbling getting louder and louder. The shed door flew open and Granny Grabbers toppled out all tangled up in sparkly material and with three sleeves accidentally knotted over her head.

'Urgent backup assistance needed,' she announced. She started to roll down the path, beeping and snatching at things with a free grabber. Then she hit a hedge and stuck there.

Delilah picked up the top hat and ran after her. 'Granny G,' she gasped, 'there's going to be something on TV about some robots from Happy Home Robotics.'

Granny Grabbers stood up carefully. She swivelled her round head from side to side. (She saw through her optical detectors, which were in the middle of her two headlamps. They looked like very large eyes.) Now she tested her fringed headlamp lids, rattling them up and down. Then she flexed each grabber in turn. Delilah untangled the sleeves of the sparkly coat and gave her back her hat.

'No damage detected,' said Granny Grabbers. 'Normal service is resumed.'

Delilah had helped her to talk a long time ago by adding bits of an old radio, a mobile phone, a television, some computers and other things to her circuits. She had her own special way of speaking.

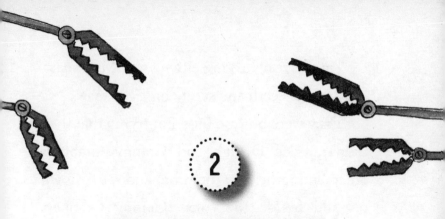

The Sort-It Squad

Mr and Mrs Smart were sitting in the living room watching the television sideways. They were watching it sideways because they were practising their arm wrestling and they were doing that because they were in training for the His and Hers Arm-Wrestling and Head-Standing Competition that was held every year at the Big Brains Institute where they worked.

'I'm not really trying,' Mr Smart was saying. 'If I tried I'd win straight away. It wouldn't be fair.'

His face was bright red. Sweat was all over it.

'I'm not really trying either,' said Mrs Smart, gritting her teeth and scrunching her eyes.

They were both so busy not trying that they didn't notice Delilah and Granny Grabbers creep and rattle into the room and settle down on and beside the sofa. (Granny Grabbers couldn't sit. She didn't bend in the middle.)

'Blingman's Department Store opened six months ago. It's the newest, biggest and most expensive store in the city,' yelled a reporter on the TV, who seemed to be standing in a car park somewhere in a strong wind.

'Blingman's have had their fair share of mysterious problems since they opened. Including a haunted lift, would you believe. But it's all good news today. The owner, Buzz Blingman, has allowed us up here on to the roof to see something you *won't* see looking around the store. No, not a beautiful display of jewellery or furnishings, although you'll find all that and more downstairs. No, we're here to see the *cleaners*.'

She was fighting with the wind. Her hair was blowing in all directions. The papers she was holding kept flapping into her face.

'This is the Sort-It Squad. The new robotic cleaning personnel made by Happy Home Robotics. They're going to be doing all the cleaning in this massive ten-storey building. And believe me, when you've seen them on parade you are going to be very, very impressed.'

Safe in the Smarts' living room, Granny Grabbers and Delilah held hand to grabber. Happy Home Robotics had made Granny Grabbers. But that was a long time ago. After that they'd made a lot of other robots, including the terrifying, shiny, two-armed, gliding, talking, laser-fingered Nanny Deluxe. Mr Smart had tried to replace Granny Grabbers with a Nanny Deluxe. It had been a time of ugliness and pain.

Even now, if Mr and Mrs Smart ever found out that Granny Grabbers had feelings and ideas of her own they would send her back to Happy Home Robotics to be re-programmed. Robots were not supposed to have feelings and ideas. (They also didn't know that she could talk.)

'What you inventing now, you monster factory,' whispered Granny Grabbers, staring ferociously at the screen.

'Why don't you give *up*, darling,' said Mrs Smart. 'You know I'll win in the end.'

'Why don't *you* give up,' said Mr Smart.

They were pulling terrible faces. Sweat was dripping off the ends of their noses. They both cared about winning more than anything else. They weren't paying any attention to the television at all.

Which meant that they were missing something rather extraordinary.

There was a squad of robots up on the rooftop car park of Blingman's Department Store. They were standing in six rows of six.

They all had the special hard hats that people wear when they are working on building sites.

'Atten-SHUN!' boomed another robot, facing them at the front. He was clearly the captain. His hat was gold instead of yellow.

'Squad RI-IGHT TURN!'

The squad turned. They were all exactly the same. Tall and shaped like cylinders with square heads and two arms each, doors on their fronts and all sorts of extra bits of equipment attached to their backs.

'Squ-ad – MARCH – LEEFT – RIGHT – LEEEFT – RIGHT,' yelled the captain at the front.

Unlike Granny Grabbers, they didn't have little wheels. They didn't float silently like the terrifying Nanny Deluxe. Instead they each had a pair of short legs and massive metal boots.

STAMP! stamped the Sort-It Squad. STAMP! STAMP! STAMP!

'RI-GHT TURN!'

They turned, they stamped, they marched up and down like the army on parade. Then they started to sing.

'We fight in the WAR on GRIME,' bellowed the captain.

'We fight GRIME all the TIME,' yelled the squad.

'Clean is GOOD and grime is BAD,
Grime's a crime, it makes us MAD,
Grime's a crime, it makes us MAD.

We fight in the WAR on MESS.
We fight MESS to EXCESS.
Any mess of any size.
We SORT IT OUT and organize.
We SORT IT OUT and ORGANIZE.'

Meanwhile the reporter had lost her pieces of paper in the wind. She was running about in the background, trying to catch them.

Delilah peered at the screen. There was something else in the background too.

Something small and almost round. And, for some reason, familiar.

It was trying to keep up with all the stamping and marching and turning. But it kept going the wrong way.

'Granny Grabbers . . .' she whispered, pointing at the screen.

Granny Grabbers beeped in shock. Her headlamps turned from calm pink to bright red.

The little round robot at the back had caught the reporter's pieces of flying paper in one of its grabbers. The reporter gave it a high-five.

The singing started again from the beginning.

'Is Pug,' whispered Granny Grabbers hoarsely.

'SQUA-AD! HA-ALT!' boomed the captain.

The squad halted. All except the little round one at the back. He had gone off the wrong way again and now his hat had fallen down over his headlamps.

Granny Grabbers beeped anxiously.

'PRO-TO-TYPE!' shouted the captain. 'HA-ALT!'

The little robot didn't seem to hear. It looked as if his hat was completely stuck. He was weaving about, tugging at it with three grabbers at once and waving the other three in the air. He crashed into the back of the squad and then bounced off several of them before bursting through the front row. Then he crashed into the captain.

The reporter was back in front of the camera, clutching her pieces of paper. 'Well, as you can see, the Sort-It Squad are the ultra-modern technological solution to the age-old problem of cleaning and—'

Her voice was drowned out by terrible shouting . . .

'You are a disgrace to Happy Home Robotics, a disgrace to the Sort-It Squad and most importantly a disgrace to ME!' The captain was towering over the little robot. Some sort of warning light seemed to be flashing where his nose would have been if he had had a nose. He looked huge and horrible.

'Ow!' squealed Delilah. Granny Grabbers was squeezing her hand so tightly it was hurting. She was also starting to roll slowly towards the television screen, pulling Delilah off the sofa as she went.

'You're an idiotic waste of metal! What are you? What are you?' yelled the captain.

'You leave him alone,' said Granny Grabbers in a low and terrible voice. 'Or you be wastey metal yourself, Rudolf.'

'Do one hundred press-ups,' continued the captain. He had only one volume, it seemed. Much Too Loud.

The reporter pulled a face at the camera. The little robot finally managed to get his hat back up off his headlamps. He really did look very, very like Granny Grabbers, except much, much smaller and even rounder. He extended two of his grabbers, leant forward and began doing press-ups.

'*We fight in the WAR on GRIME!*' began the captain, his red nose still flashing nastily.

'*We fight GRIME all the TIME!*' answered the squad, stamping very hard.

'. . . And now we'll go back downstairs to see the excellent furniture department . . .' yelled the reporter. 'And don't forget, Blingman's will be open late on Saturday for its Late-Night Easter Extravaganza.'

'I WIN!' shouted Mr and Mrs Smart, both at exactly the same time. The table they were leaning on had broken. They were in a heap on the floor.

Delilah didn't notice. She was far too worried. Granny Grabbers' headlamps were their most angry colour of all – bright lime green. She had finally let go of Delilah's hand. She was standing very close to the television screen wringing all three pairs of her grabbers, beeping and muttering very softly.

'Darling, you know I won,' Mrs Smart was saying from somewhere behind the sofa. 'You broke the table on purpose.'

'I did not break the table,' said Mr Smart. 'I haven't broken anything since I broke the washing machine last Tuesday when I was improving it . . .'

'Granny Grabbers?' whispered Delilah.

Granny Grabbers turned her headlamps towards her. Delilah swallowed. 'Are you all right, Granny?'

'Mr Smart has prepared toads-in-their-holes,' said Granny Grabbers. 'Child Unit go and have tea. Grabbers must have period of deep multi-thought.'

'What is it?' said Delilah, following her past her parents, still arguing on the floor, and out of the room. And down the hall.

'Grabbers major shock,' said Granny Grabbers. 'If holey toad taste bad have something from fridge.'

'Yes, yes.' Delilah didn't feel hungry, for toads or anything else. 'But what's wrong? Is it to do with that little robot? The one who looked like you?'

'Grabbers must think now,' said Granny Grabbers. 'Child Unit will get news update at bedtime.'

She patted Delilah on her shoulder with a shaky grabber, opened the cupboard under the stairs and went inside among the brooms and buckets. The door closed behind her.

Delilah heard a click and a thud. This was the sound of the door at the back of the cupboard. The door to Granny Grabbers' own secret and private room.

She thought she heard a burst of music, very muffled. That would be Granny Grabbers putting on her massive headphones so that she could listen to the sound that she found most relaxing in a crisis. The crashing and wailing of her favourite band – the Dentists of Doom.

3

Escaping the Toad-In-The-Hole

Delilah was feeling terrible. She tried to eat some of Mr Smart's toad-in-the-hole but she wasn't hungry. She kept thinking about the Sort-It Squad. How big were those robots? Two metres tall at least. And how big was the little one who was in all the trouble? She thought that he was a little bit smaller than she was herself. He was a little, round version of Granny Grabbers . . .

'Are you enjoying my delicious gourmet amphibian recipe?' asked Mr Smart, coming into the kitchen carrying a piece of the broken arm-wrestling table.

'It's got sixteen different herbs and spices. It's the only toad-in-the-hole recipe that has fresh fig and garlic in the batter.'

Mr Smart had recently become very keen on cooking. He had bought a smoothie maker, a pasta maker and a bread maker. (Mrs Smart had suggested he try and buy a mess maker as well and then screamed with laughter and said that he didn't need to because mess was the only thing that he could make himself.) He had three different aprons and a chef's hat, all hanging on special hooks.

'I'm not really hungry,' said Delilah.

'Your mother's broken this table,' said Mr Smart. 'I'm going to get my tools from the garage.'

He swerved out through the utility room, knocking over a plant in a pot with the piece of table.

Delilah quickly opened the fridge. It was

crammed with all sorts of ingredients for Mr Smart's experimental recipes. However, there were some lunchboxes in a neat pile at the back. Granny Grabbers had put them there for her and they were all full of things she liked. She took the top one, closed the fridge and hurried outside, leaving the fig and garlic toad-in-the-hole on the table.

A moment later and she was cosy in the shed. The lunchbox contained a hard-boiled egg, a fruit salad and a piece of Granny Grabbers' grabber-made sticky chocolate cake with sticky chocolate icing. As usual, Granny Grabbers had put a joke in there too. A bit like the sort you get in Christmas crackers. Her jokes were always written on a scrap of paper in spiky grabberwriting and she had always invented them herself.

'Why is there a dent in the shed?' read Delilah out loud to Dr Doomy. 'Because Dr Doomy is a gerbil and a gerbil is a rodent.'

Delilah rolled her eyes. So did Dr Doomy.

'She's shut herself in her secret room,' said Delilah. 'She's ever so upset.' And she gave him a piece of banana. It was a lovely fruit salad, but she still didn't really feel like eating. She was too worried about Granny Grabbers.

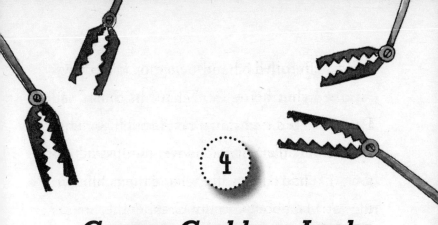

4

Granny Grabbers Looks at a Photograph

Meanwhile, Granny Grabbers was in her secret room hidden at the back of the cupboard under the stairs. She moved her laptop to the side of her worktable. Then she reached down with three grabbers, prised up a loose floorboard and, very carefully, lifted a shoebox out from the space under the floor. She put it on the table and wiped away some dust.

She stayed still for a moment, bathed in the pale-green light of her lava lamp, looking at the closed box. No one else knew about this box. Not even Delilah.

She lifted the lid and began to take things out one by one. The form that Mrs Smart had signed when the postman first brought Granny Grabbers to the Smarts' house; the instruction book that had come with her and the number to ring, at Happy Home Robotics, if the Smarts ever thought there was a problem. All kept here in this box, safe where Mr and Mrs Smart would never find them.

Underneath all this there was a photograph. It was wrapped in a bit of tissue paper.

Granny Grabbers unwrapped it slowly. Then she stared at it for a long time. It was the little robot who was now such an unlikely member of the Sort-It Squad. He was standing in what looked like a storeroom. There were boxes and crates all around, most of them with Happy Home Robotics stamped on the side.

The robot was standing next to a small table. It looked as if someone had just finished a game of dominoes. The dominoes were still there, neatly laid out.

He was holding a sealed wooden crate above his head. It was big. At least three times as big as he was. He had kept a grabber free to wave to the camera. His headlamps were a triumphant, gleeful red.

Granny Grabbers stared at the photograph for a long time. She tapped it gently with a grabber. Delilah had been quite right. The little robot did look very like her. Except he was much smaller and rounder. And there was something else too – he had writing on his side. Or, at least, the remains of some writing. The last part had worn off. The bit that was left said 'Prototype Undergoing . . .'

She turned the photograph over. There was grabber-type writing on the back. Very like her own, but even spikier.

yor
frend
pug
xxx

5

Message from Babbatunde

It was getting late. Delilah went up to her room, past Mr and Mrs Smart, who were now standing on their heads in the hall.

'You should do this, Delilah,' said Mr Smart. She couldn't see his face because his jumper had slipped down, but from the sound of his voice she imagined it was the colour of a beetroot.

'It's good for the brain,' gasped Mrs Smart. 'My hearing has improved already, just since I've been here now. I can even hear some music coming from next door.'

'It's OK, thanks,' said Delilah, glancing

anxiously at the door to the cupboard under the stairs. They were very near to it. She had a nasty feeling that a certain robot's headphones must be leaking again.

Her bedroom had recently been grabber-painted pale blue with a beautiful, slightly square grabber-made cushion and grabber-embroidered curtains in dark blue and yellow. There were supposed to be sunflowers on the curtains, although most of them looked like bunches of bananas and one looked more like a tractor. Delilah didn't care. She thought they were probably the nicest curtains in the world.

Sir Isaac Newton, the Brain Building Alphabet Bear, was sitting on the chest of drawers.

'Granny Grabbers is very upset,' Delilah told him. 'She saw this little robot on television getting shouted at. He's working in that big new shop, Blingman's. I think he's a relative from when she was at Happy Home Robotics.'

She hugged Sir Isaac tightly round his middle.

'T is for text message,' he growled. He had been given to Delilah when she was little and he was supposed to say things like 'A is for apple', but he was very much his own bear.

Delilah groaned. Of course, she had left her mobile phone on the bed and then forgotten all about it. She picked it up.

'Oh great! It's from Babbatunde. Listen to this.'

Over here staying at embassy. Shopping
2moro + mum 4 shoes. U meet us?
MayB shoes scared of bears. B

Babbatunde was Delilah's best friend. His father was the President of the Island of Amania off the west coast of Africa. His mother was a famous singer. She was big and beautiful and loved shoes. Babbatunde had spent ages waiting in shoe shops all over the world.

'Brilliant,' whispered Delilah. 'We'll tell him all about Granny Grabbers being upset. And Sofia always loves to see you, doesn't she.'

She hugged Sir Isaac again.

'L is for lovely,' he muttered dreamily.

'But you don't even *wear* shoes,' said Delilah.

Sir Isaac remained mysterious behind his big green-framed glasses.

6

Granny Grabbers Takes the Curtains

There was a familiar thudding sound and the house shook slightly. Granny Grabbers couldn't go upstairs on her little wheels, of course. She used springs. BOING! Thump! BOING! Thump! Then the comforting rattling noise as she came down the passageway. Finally the tap of a grabber on the door.

'Warm milk and news update,' she said, rolling into the room. 'Followed by tonight's story at bedtime starting in five minutes.' She was wearing her pink flannelette nightcap.

'Babbatunde's mum is shopping in town

tomorrow,' said Delilah quickly. 'He's invited me and Sir Isaac to go too. We could go and check out Blingman's Department Store. We might see your friend.'

At the mention of Blingman's, Granny Grabbers clenched all her grabbers, including the one holding the mug of warm milk. Waves started crashing about in there. The milk began slopping over the sides.

Delilah took it. Granny Grabbers clenched that grabber so hard it made a crunching noise.

'Child Unit observed small robot in silly stompy-stomp cleanage parade?'

'Yes, of course, that's who I—'

'Is Grabbers' old friend.'

'Yes, I realized—'

'Is very dear secret and oldest friend. From history.'

'Yes, I guessed—'

'In the early history of Grabbers, Grabbers lived at the Happy Home Robotics. Grabbers and Pug secret friends at night. When bossy robot scientist-humans gone home.'

'Yes,' said Delilah.

'Then Grabbers comes to live with Smart family to care for Child Unit. To provide love, wisdom, fruit, vegetables and chocolate cake.'

'Yes,' said Delilah.

'Regular exercise is also important. Always cleans teeths.'

Delilah nodded.

'Child Unit most precious thing in world. Child Unit heartmost.'

Delilah nodded again. This was getting intense.

'Pug like little brother to Grabbers.'

Granny Grabbers removed her nightcap and took a photograph from inside it. She held it out to Delilah. It was the one she had been looking at in her secret room.

'Prototype Under . . . going . . .' whispered Delilah. 'P – U – g . . . What does that mean?

Prototype Undergoing . . . what?'

'Tests, experiments. Making very strong robot. Pug very strong. Now Happy Home Robotics finished tests. They have sold him. No doubty for heavy lifting to help in cleanage.' Her headlamps flashed a truly terrifying lime green.

'Grabbers must rescue. We regret to announce that Grabbers will need curtains.'

'Curtains? You mean my curtains? My new ones?'

'In order to remain hush-hush secretive, other curtains must go on as normally opening and shutting.'

Granny Grabbers sailed over to the window, took the beautiful banana and tractor curtains down very quickly, using all grabbers, and then hung a blanket over the rail instead.

Delilah sank back on to the bed and put down her milk. Once Granny Grabbers had an idea, however crazy it might be, there was no way of stopping her.

'Child Unit to investigate Blingman's Department Store tomorrow. Locate all stairs and lifts and back door and fire escape. Grabbers home in garage.'

'But what . . . why are you going to be in the garage?'

'Building getaway grabbmobile. Using old motorbike sadly neglected by Mr Smart.'

'WHAT? It's NOT neglected. And it's NOT old. That's his new special motorbike for going on holiday next summer.'

Mr Smart had indeed bought himself a huge and expensive motorbike with heated seats, a music system and a big storage box on the back. It was under a special sheet in the garage and Delilah was not allowed to touch it.

'You can't ride it. You don't even know how.'

She hugged Sir Isaac tightly.

'L is for licence,' he informed them mournfully. 'P is for police.'

Granny Grabbers snorted.

'Story to commence in thirty seconds,' she said, picking a book off the shelf. 'Pirates. To get us in mood for daring deeds and big much bravery.'

Delilah could read perfectly well. However, she and Granny Grabbers still enjoyed a bedtime story together.

Tonight it was a wild and scary business about some pirates rescuing another pirate from a desert island. Then Delilah lay in bed, staring at the blanket over the window, and listening to the sounds of goodness knew what going on in the garage.

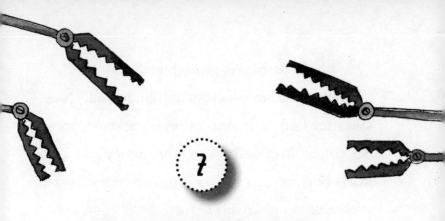

Moonlight Mystery

It was the next morning. Delilah and Granny Grabbers were dithering about at the front door, waiting for Babbatunde and his mother to arrive. Sir Isaac Newton was waiting too, with his silvery-grey fur beautifully brushed and his glasses freshly polished.

'I don't like to leave you when you're so upset,' said Delilah.

'Grabbers has more building work to do,' said Granny Grabbers, worryingly. She hadn't let Delilah look inside the garage yet.

'*Building*? I thought we were just going to,

you know, *borrow* his motorbike.'

'Child Unit investigate Blingman's. Note location fire escapes. Mobile phone charge uttermost and full of creddy money? In case Grabbers needs send message or communicate verbally.'

'Yes.' Delilah's heart sank. Granny Grabbers didn't use the phone very much and when she did, it was usually rather alarming.

'Good. And is also good to spend time with friend own age and species. Shared interest and laughter boosty immune system. Have cleaned teeths?'

'Yes, yes, really.'

A large black car with the Amanian flag on the bonnet pulled up at the gate. Babbatunde's mother, Sofia, stepped out first, wearing the Amanian national costume and looking gorgeous.

'Granny G. How are you, my dear? And Delilah . . . let me give you a hug. Oh, you've grown . . .'

She wrapped her arms around Delilah and Sir Isaac, and lifted them right off the ground.

'B is for beautiful,' whispered a shy, husky voice from somewhere inside the hug.

Babbatunde bounced on to the path. He grinned at Delilah. Then Granny Grabbers hugged him and he disappeared in a tangle of grabbers.

As soon as all the greetings were over Granny Grabbers began wringing her grabbers together. Her headlamps turned a sorrowful blue.

'Are you all right, my dear?' asked Sofia, putting a hand on one of Granny Grabbers' various shoulders.

Granny Grabbers made a noise that sounded a bit like a sniff.

'Grabbers thanks for concern. Health status good. Much work to do today. Child Unit to be returned approximately seventeen hundred five o'clock hours?'

'Of course,' said Sofia. 'Are you sure you

don't want to join us, Granny G?'

Granny Grabbers shook her head. 'Grabbers has urgent work,' she said. 'In the garage.'

'In the garage?' said Sofia, raising her perfect eyebrows. 'What are you doing in there?'

Granny Grabbers lowered her headlamp lids.

'Much urgent work,' she said. 'Do you have a chainsaw I could borrow?'

Delilah and Babbatunde exchanged glances.

'Not in the car,' said Sofia, who was not easily shocked. 'But I can ask our chauffeur to go and buy you one while we are in Blingman's. Is there anything else you need?'

Granny Grabbers' headlamps flashed red with excitement. Mr Adeleye the chauffeur was a good friend of hers. She had recently made a satnav for him featuring her own voice.

'Grabbers will provide money,' she said. 'Assistance greatly appreciated. Two tins black paint for outdoor woodwork. Ten metres furry material grey, brown, pink or blue. Three pairs bunny ears assorted sizes. Many little chocolate eggs.'

'I'll write it all down,' said Sofia, getting a pen out of her handbag.

A few minutes later Babbatunde, Delilah, Sir Isaac and Sofia all climbed into the back of the car. The smell of perfume was so strong Delilah was surprised that she couldn't see it hovering about in the air.

'M is for Moonlight,' growled Sir Isaac softly as they glided off down the road. 'And mystery.'

'Oh, he's so sweet,' cooed Sofia, opening her handbag. 'He even recognizes my scent.' She took out a heart-shaped bottle with 'Moonlight Mystery' written on the side and dabbed a little drop on Sir Isaac's paw. He didn't say anything, but his glasses misted over.

'The mystery is how anyone can breathe,' said Babbatunde.

'Blingman Brothers have a wonderful shoe

department in New York, but it's so far away, we don't go there very often,' said Sofia, ignoring him. 'There are two Blingman brothers, I believe, Vinnie and Buzz, but I do not think they get on very well. I am very pleased that Buzz Blingman decided to come over here and open a store of his own. Now we'll be able to buy lovely shoes whenever we come to the city.'

Babbatunde groaned.

'They've got ten floors, I think,' said Delilah. 'And a car park on the roof. I'm really hoping to have a good look round. I want to see everything. The lifts, the stairs, the fire exits . . .'

She trailed off. Sofia and Babbatunde were both staring at her.

'We could count the toilets,' said Babbatunde. 'That sounds like fun too.'

She pulled a face at him.

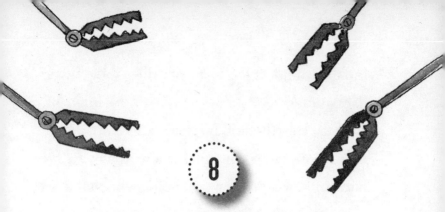

8

Shoes and Phones

Blingman's did have a lot of shoes – and when they saw Babbatunde's mother they started getting them all out to show her.

'Please would you sign this for my wife,' asked the manager of the shoe department, holding out a shoebox lid. 'She loves all your music. Especially your new album *Songbird of Amania*. We both do.'

Sofia sat down and was soon surrounded by piles of boxes and tissue paper and very expensive shoes in all sorts of colours.

'Me and Delilah thought we'd have a quick

look around the rest of the shop,' said Babbatunde.

'Stay together, do not leave the shop, do not talk to strangers and make sure that you are back in half an hour,' said Sofia, who was a lot more organized than people expected.

'Sir Isaac can stay with me, if he likes.' She picked up Sir Isaac and cuddled him.

'B is for bliss,' he mumbled in an unusually squeaky voice.

'If Madam wishes to look at a matching pair of shoes for her bear companion . . .' began the manager, eyeing Sir Isaac enviously. 'Or perhaps a small jacket?'

'And B is for back off, buster,' said Sir Isaac.

Babbatunde and Delilah hurried away. Out of shoes, through handbags, deep into umbrellas and parasols.

'Tell me immediately what is going on, why Granny G needs a chainsaw and some Easter

46

eggs, and the reason for your sudden interest in lifts and stairs,' hissed Babbatunde.

'My dad broke his chainsaw trying to saw through the lamppost outside our house. The light kept flickering on and off one night and it was keeping him awake—'

'Tell me, NOW, what is GOING ON!'

So Delilah told Babbatunde all about Pug and the Sort-It Squad and their horrible captain and the photograph of Pug taken during the Early History of Granny Grabbers. Then, before he had time to speak, she told him about the plan to rescue Pug and about the grabbmobile currently under construction in the garage.

Babbatunde whistled through his teeth.

Delilah picked up a pink polka-dot parasol with a flamingo-head handle. She was sure Granny Grabbers would love it.

'Can I help you, Madam?' asked an assistant.

'It's OK,' said Delilah. The flamingo parasol was far too expensive.

'It's the dots,' whispered Babbatunde. 'They're a pound each. And this is really cool, by the way. Another Granny Grabbers action adventure. Starting now.' He grinned.

'It's *serious*,' whispered Delilah. 'I really want us to rescue him, of course I do. I just don't want anyone to be, you know, *arrested* or something. If Granny Grabbers ever gets into trouble, any at all, she'll get sent straight back to Happy Home Robotics *for ever*.'

'No one is going to arrest Granny G,' said Babbatunde. 'It would be like arresting a battleship.'

They had reached the escalators. The furniture department was straight ahead through an archway. The lights were dimmed in there. Strange shapes loomed in the gloom. There was a row of plastic chairs and a piece of tape across the entrance with a sign saying: 'Closed to the public'.

Then, suddenly, there was a strange crashing

noise. Like someone dropping a plate. Or maybe two plates.

Babbatunde looked round in alarm. So did several very expensive-looking ladies who were just stepping off the escalator.

The crash turned into splashing, gurgling and rattling. Delilah pulled her mobile phone out of her pocket and the sound became louder. Her ringtone was a recording she had made of Granny Grabbers doing the washing-up.

'Hello, Granny,' said Delilah.

There was a tremendous bang and then some very high-pitched whistling. Delilah held the phone at arm's length. The whistling grew even louder and terribly piercing. She knew what had happened. Granny Grabbers had accidentally hit herself on the side of the head with the phone. She often did this.

At last. Silence.

Then some disgruntled beeping.

Delilah cautiously moved the phone a bit nearer to her ear.

'Granny Grabbers, are you there?'

Meanwhile, Babbatunde nodded politely to several people who had stopped to stare.

'Special mobile,' he said. 'We're really only supposed to use it underwater.'

Delilah frowned at the phone. Now it had started buzzing. Then she made out Granny Grabbers' voice. It rattled and echoed as if she had a bucket over her head.

(It is important to remember that, unlike robots who have been built to talk, Granny Grabbers did not have a loudspeaker to the outside. Her voice came mainly out of her chest and in all directions. She also had a habit of waving the phone about as she talked instead of keeping it near the auditory detectors on the side of her head. All this made phone conversations very unpredictable.)

'Rescue mission tonight during Late-Night

Easter Extragander,' she said. 'Child Unit state current location.'

'What?' squeaked Delilah.

'She wants to know where we are,' hissed Babbatunde. 'It's a school project,' he added to a Blingman's assistant who had arrived beside them and didn't seem to want to go. 'This is an antique mobile phone. We're testing the signal. My mother is buying a lot of shoes.'

'Blingman's,' said Delilah, trying to whisper.

'Excellent,' barked Granny Grabbers. 'Child Unit has seen Pug?'

'No.' Delilah was trying to muffle Granny Grabbers' voice by pushing the phone up her sleeve and talking to her through a layer of jumper. 'He's probably, you know, having a rest in the basement or somewhere like that during the daytime.'

Granny Grabbers beeped to herself. 'Pug understand speech,' she shouted after a moment's reflection. 'But Pug only speak Morsel.'

'What? You don't need to talk so loud, Granny. I can hear everything you're saying. Everybody can. I just don't know what Morsel—'

'Child Unit make map. Fire exit. Lifts. Tip bang stairs.'

'Yes, we will. We are—' said Delilah.

'Child Unit beware of tip bang stairs.'

'Yes. Of course.'

'I think Queen Victoria may have had a phone like this,' Babbatunde told yet another assistant. 'They always put them in their sleeves in those days. It was considered more polite. That's why you don't see them with phones in the photographs.'

'Tip bang stairs much big madness, approach with due care and attention at all times,' continued Granny Grabbers at enormous volume. She seemed to feel very strongly on the matter.

Delilah tried to reply. She had lifted her arm

too high and the phone had slipped right past her elbow.

'We have to go,' she muttered desperately into her armpit. 'Everyone's looking.'

'Tip bang stairs health warning,' bellowed Granny Grabbers. 'Over and out Roger.'

Delilah stepped backwards into a woman carrying a lot of Blingman's bags.

'Sorry,' she mumbled, trying to get the phone out of her jumper and getting both her arms stuck in the same sleeve. 'It's my granny.'

The woman smiled a little nervous smile and hurried away.

'Stop laughing,' said Delilah to Babbatunde. 'And before you ask – tip bang stairs are escalators. Granny G doesn't find them very easy because they're not the right shape for her. She's had a couple of bad experiences involving tipping over and falling all the way down.'

'I worked that out,' said Babbatunde. 'But what's this about Pug speaking Morsel? Do you know what that is?'

Delilah shook her head and shrugged. She and Babbatunde had met when their parents had entered them into the Worldwide Junior Extreme General Knowledge Competition. They had both learnt a great many facts for that competition. What Morsel was, and how to speak it, wasn't among them.

'No time to guess now,' said Babbatunde quickly. 'I think your sergeant-major friend is coming our way.'

Delilah had her back towards the entrance to the furniture department. She spun round . . .

Several people were emerging from the gloom and stepping over the tape. There was a man in a dark suit who was rubbing his hands together anxiously and talking at the same time. There was also a larger man, dressed in a Blingman's uniform and dark glasses; two children, a boy and a girl; and a small frowning woman with a briefcase. Finally, towering over them all – stomping and swaying beside them – was a very tall robot with a cylindrical body, two huge feet, two long arms and a gold hard hat. The captain of the Sort-It Squad.

Delilah and Babbatunde concealed themselves in a display of open umbrellas.

9

Secrecy Code 9

'We must make absolutely sure that the press don't get hold of this,' said the man in the suit, biting several of his fingernails. 'Absolutely no one must find out. Especially not my brother Vinnie. If he finds out he'll tell everyone. People will laugh at us. Globally. They will laugh at us globally on a global scale.'

'Yes, Mr Blingman,' said the large man and the frowning woman.

'If my brother finds out that one of our new robot cleaners – which we were showing off on primetime television only yesterday – has built an obstacle course out of thousands of pounds' worth of furniture during the night—'

'Yes, Mr Blingman, of course,' said the woman. They could see her badge now: **Miss Treen. Furniture Specialist**.

'Affirmative, Mr Blingman,' said the big man in dark glasses. His badge said: **Head of Security**. 'Secrecy Code 9. I will instruct all units.'

'Shouldn't it be Code 10?'

'With respect, Mr Blingman, a Code 10 secret is one that no one knows.'

'But that's what I want. I want no one to know.'

'With respect, Mr Blingman, sir, *we* know. But rest assured, sir, Code 9 is a very high code. Code 10s almost never happen because we don't know we don't know them so we don't give them a code. Sir.'

Mr Blingman shook his head from side to side like a dog trying to dry its ears. Then he craned his neck to look up at the captain. 'ANYWAY, I want all this, this *mess*, tidied up at once. Can we do that?'

'Sir, yes, Mr Blingman, sir, yes, sir!' yelled the captain, causing everyone else to jump and step backwards. 'It will take the squad about eight hours, sir!'

'But I thought you said the little prototype did it all by itself during the night,' said Mr Blingman.

'Sir, Mr Blingman, sir, yes, sir! Prototype is the only squad member strong enough! Prototype is as strong as six other Sort-It Squad members put together, sir!'

'Well, get the prototype to clear this up then.'

'Sir, Mr Blingman, sir! At the moment Prototype has gone absent without leave, sir!'

'Why on earth aren't you looking for it then?'

'I'm afraid that's because I instructed them not to, Mr Blingman,' said Miss Treen the

Furniture Specialist. 'I thought that the squad members might alarm the customers. Or stand on them accidentally. I asked the captain to postpone the search until tonight.'

The captain saluted violently. 'Sir, Mr—'

'*Please*, Captain, don't say anything else for a moment.' Mr Blingman had covered his ears with his hands. 'My head is ringing . . .'

'Sir, yes, Mr Bling—' began the captain, before he managed to stop himself.

Mr Blingman very slowly removed one of his hands from one of his ears and pulled some blue worry beads out of his pocket. He began running them backwards and forwards through his fingers so fast they became a blue blur. He had clearly had a lot of practice at worrying.

Then he turned to face the two children who were looking very cute and very grumpy at the same time.

'Dollie and Billie. Go upstairs and look

around the toy department. My assistant will come with you.'

The boy and the girl both shrugged their shoulders, rolled their eyes and raised their eyebrows.

'We're SO-O-O bored,' they said in unison.

'I want a puppy,' said Dollie. 'To dress up in little puppy clothes and carry around with me. *Everybody else* has got one.'

'I want an alligator,' said Billie. '*No one* else has got one of those.'

'Now, Dollie, you know your mother doesn't allow animals in any of our houses,' said Mr Blingman rather wearily. 'And, Billie, *you* know she doesn't allow animals in any of our swimming pools.'

'I want a puppy for my birthday,' said Dollie.

'I want an alligator,' said Billie.

'Go up to the toy department. It's on the top floor next to the café,' said Mr Blingman. 'And pick out a toy each.'

'I want two things,' said Dollie.

'So do I,' said Billie. 'You said it would be fun coming to the store with you today. It's been the most bo-oring thing I've ever done . . .'

'Yes, well, not everything's gone according to plan,' said Mr Blingman, glancing back into the darkened furniture department.

'You should have let us go on that slide,' said Dollie.

'Run along,' said Mr Blingman, wiping his forehead. 'That was not a slide. It was a very expensive table and some very, very expensive sofas. That robot is certainly strong.'

'He sounds really cool,' said Billie. 'Even cooler than an alligator.'

Delilah and Babbatunde remained absolutely still behind the biggest umbrella as the twins ducked towards them under the security tape.

'I bet a robot would make a great pet,' Billie was saying to Dollie.

'Only if it was a cute robot,' said Dollie. 'This one's probably really ugly. Like the captain . . .'

And they both burst into snorts and giggles and imitated the captain's stomping walk as far as the escalator.

10

Deep in the Furniture Department

'I'm going up to the office to phone these Happy Home Robotic people and complain,' said Mr Blingman. 'They can come and fetch this prototype as soon as we find it. And I'm going to get my camera. We need proof.'

Miss Treen nodded earnestly, clutching her briefcase to her chest. The captain snapped to attention, making the floor shake, and saluted and—

'Don't speak!' cried Mr Blingman, just in time.

They walked, and stomped, past the display

of big umbrellas and out of sight round the corner.

A big group of customers came past, laughing and talking. They stopped and told each other how disappointed they were that the furniture department was closed and how much they thought they should go upstairs for coffee and cake.

When they had all gone, Delilah and Babbatunde crept into view at last. They dodged quickly under the security tape and stole into the dark.

Gradually their eyes adjusted: huge shapes rose up all around them.

'Look at that,' whispered Babbatunde.

'It's a pile of chairs,' said Delilah.

They weren't the sort of chairs people normally put into piles, like school chairs. They were great big soft comfy armchairs piled up right to the ceiling.

'And look, sofas!'

There was indeed a pile of sofas. Six of them, one on top of the other. Like enormous crooked steps.

'I think this is the slide . . . the one those kids wanted to go on,' whispered Delilah.

'You mean the Blingman twins, Dollar and Bill?'

'Is that really what they're called?'

'Yeah. Mum told me. She read it in *Yadda Yadda* magazine. They do adverts for shampoo and— Oh WOW!'

They had found the slide itself. A huge dining table was tilted on end against the top of the sofa pile. It was very, very polished and shiny. If it had been standing as normal on the floor, twenty people could easily have fitted around it. But it wasn't standing on the floor as normal at all. And all you had to do was climb up to the top of the sofas and then . . .

'Let's try it,' said Babbatunde.

They both started hauling themselves up

from one sofa to the next. Babbatunde got to the top first, lost his footing, shot down the table sideways and landed in a heap next to a giant pyramid made out of cushions.

Delilah   followed,
upside down.

As soon as they had disentangled themselves they ran round to climb back up.

They had almost reached the top again when all the lights in the furniture department suddenly came on at once.

There were voices. One of them was definitely Buzz Blingman.

Clutching on to each other, Delilah and Babbatunde fell down the slide in a lump and crawled towards the nearest possible hiding place. A gap in the bottom of the pyramid of cushions. It was hollow in there, like a den.

They stayed inside, keeping well back in the shadow and peering out.

Buzz Blingman and Miss Treen came right up to the pyramid and stopped. Buzz was carrying a very big camera and some sort of spotlight. Miss Treen was struggling with a tripod.

'It obviously built itself an obstacle course,' said Buzz. 'Put the tripod here, would you? We want a good picture of the slide.'

'The maze made out of cupboards is over there,' said Miss Treen. 'It's a very clever design, sir.'

'We'll take a picture of this cushion pyramid-thing next and then the pile of pianos,' continued Buzz, who was clearly too wound up to listen. 'Three pianos one on top of the other. Sort of musical climbing frame. I think that's what alerted the rest of the squad. They left the prototype in here to move a few things around and they heard all this binging and bonging and twanging. The only way to climb it is by standing on the strings.'

The camera buzzed and clicked.

'You're new here, aren't you?' said Buzz. 'We've had problems from the moment we opened. I suspect they've been the work of my brother, Vinnie. He's determined to close me down. He let loose a lot of rats in our ladies' underwear department a week after we opened. Thank goodness it wasn't spiders. I hate spiders.'

'Oh, Mr Blingman, surely he wouldn't.'

'He most certainly would. It's dog eat dog in this business,' said Buzz. 'Or in that case, rat eat knickers. We had to close the whole place down for two days.'

Delilah and Babbatunde cringed back as Buzz and Miss Treen walked past the small opening to the pyramid.

Buzz stopped. He seemed to be doing something to the camera.

'He comes over in secret in his private jet and puts on disguises,' Buzz went on. 'He pretended to be a lift engineer after the business with the rats. He planted a little tape machine that made a sinister giggling noise when anyone pressed the button for Floor Nine, Carpets and Bedding. No one bought a duvet or a rug for weeks.'

'Oh, Mr Blingman, goodness me.'

'He's Mom's favourite,' said Buzz. 'He picked on me all the time when we were kids and he's still picking on me now. He's older, bigger and better-looking than me and he always gets his own way.'

There was a sudden extraordinary sound. What was it? Yes. It was an animal of some sort. An animal snarling. It sounded like a lion. Usually safely confined to wildlife programmes on the television. Getting louder . . .

'WHAT on EARTH is THAT?' yelled Buzz. He grabbed Miss Treen's arm and they looked all around, wild-eyed.

Babbatunde was scrabbling to try and get at his phone. He accidentally rolled on to it. The lion started to roar . . .

'IS THAT A LION? WHERE is it COMING FROM?' cried Buzz.

Babbatunde had got the phone tangled up in his shoulder bag. He couldn't see it. He could only feel it. He thumped frantically at it anyway, trying to get the off button. He missed.

'It's coming from in there, sir,' cried Miss Treen. 'I'll call security—'

'No time! A lion loose in the shop could close us down for good! I am trained in martial arts. I am a Black Sock and a BashaNosa Master Level Twelve—'

Babbatunde had hit the right button.

Silence.

Delilah and Babbatunde crawled to the back of the pyramid, as far from the little opening as possible.

'I think maybe it was a *recording* of a lion,' whispered Miss Treen very politely.

'Do you think so?' whispered Buzz.

'Well, it seems more likely, sir. It did stop rather abruptly ... and then it made a sort of beeping noise as well.'

Another pause.

'Vinnie has done this, for sure,' hissed Buzz. 'He's planted this, this lion noise somewhere in here. I realized that it wasn't a real lion, of course, from the start. You don't think he could have had anything to do with the prototype that's caused all this trouble, do you? Whose idea was it to hire this Sort-It Squad to do the cleaning, anyway?'

'Yours, Mr Blingman,' said Miss Treen promptly.

'Yes, well, obviously it was a great idea of mine. I guess that's one problem Vinnie hasn't caused. But he *has* planted this lion noise and we need to find it right now.'

Delilah and Babbatunde started to burrow between the cushions at the back of the pyramid. The entire pyramid rocked from side to side.

'He's in there! I'll handle this!' yelled Buzz.

He dived head first into the pyramid just as Delilah was pulling Babbatunde out through the back wall (his trainer had got caught on something).

The pyramid collapsed inwards.

'Don't think you can get away, Vinnie!' mumbled Buzz, now completely buried.

'I'll get you out of there, sir,' cried Miss Treen, throwing herself after him.

'You've just put your foot in my mouth; it's not helpful . . .' shouted Buzz, much muffled. The whole mountain of cushions was moving. Bits of Mr Blingman and Miss Treen appeared through the surface and disappeared again.

Delilah and Babbatunde hesitated, ran towards the taped-off entrance, saw a security man walking past, ran back . . . and bundled each other into the maze.

It was made of winding rows of cupboards and bookcases and wardrobes. All much too tall for them to see over the top. They turned a few corners and then stopped running and looked at each other.

They could still hear Buzz Blingman.

'Call security and get them to do a thorough

search of the building. Look for my brother Vinnie, who will probably be in disguise. Also for bugs, microphones and tiny hidden devices making noises like lions. They're probably going off all over the store at this moment, terrifying customers.'

Their voices were getting fainter. They were hurrying away.

The lights in the furniture department went out again.

11

In the Cupboard Maze

Delilah and Babbatunde sat down on the floor in the dark.

'We've got to find him before they do,' whispered Delilah.

Babbatunde was texting his mother. 'That was her,' he said anxiously. 'We should have been back by now. I'm just saying we've got a bit delayed. Then I'll use our secret word. So she knows it's really me . . .'

He had finished the text and stared past Delilah, up at the ceiling. He put his finger to his lips and pointed.

Delilah turned and looked.

There was a bluish patch of light on the ceiling above what looked to be the middle of the maze. It was flashing on and off.

They watched for a moment longer, then Babbatunde suddenly punched the air and grinned.

He leant forward and whispered in Delilah's ear.

'It's Morse code. Get it? Morsel is Morse. Don't you recognize it? It's the international distress signal. Dah-dah-dah. Di-di-di. Dah-dah-dah . . .'

Delilah got it at once. She'd heard of Morse code. It was used to send radio messages. Each letter of the alphabet was a different pattern of long and short beeps. She watched the flashing light.

'S.O.S.,' she whispered.

Babbatunde nodded. 'It's Pug. It's him. He's got a torch or something and he's sending a message in Morsel. He's here.'

Without another word they both stood up and began to creep forward. It was very dark. They went very slowly. They went round one corner, and another. They came to a dead end. They went back and turned the other way.

Gradually, with a lot of wrong turnings, they grew nearer to the flashing light.

And then suddenly they were in the middle of the maze.

The blue light swung down from the ceiling and shone straight in their faces, dazzling them both.

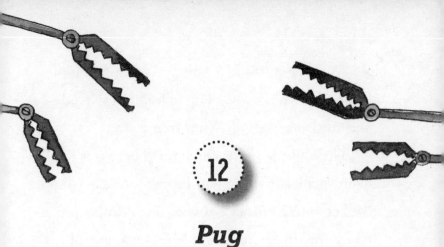

12

Pug

'Is that you, Pug?' said Delilah. 'We've come to rescue you.'

The torch beam wobbled a bit, as if the person holding it was not sure what to do.

'Granny Grabbers saw you on the television—' began Babbatunde.

'That's no good,' hissed Delilah. 'Granny wasn't *called* Granny Grabbers then, was she? Not before she came to live at our house.'

'Well, what *was* she called before that?'

Delilah frantically tried to think of the answer.

'Mark 1,' she said. 'Mark 1. At Happy Home Robotics. You know, Pug. Dominoes. And – and six arms like you. Your friend . . .'

Then all the lights came on. There was Pug, even smaller than he had looked on television, backed into a corner between a wardrobe and a fancy-looking bookcase. He was waving all his grabbers in front of his headlamps and beeping very quietly.

Now they could hear voices. The captain of the Sort-It Squad, shouting orders. 'SQ-UUAD, HALT! SQ-UUAD, CO-OM-MENCE SE-EARCH!'

'We fight in the war on grime!'

'We fight grime all the time!'

Pug stopped waving. He dropped the torch. He looked from Delilah to Babbatunde and back again. His headlamps were purple with fear.

'Oh no,' groaned Delilah.

'Let's hide him under our coats.' Babbatunde started pulling his own coat off.

'Don't be crazy, he's not *that* small.'

The tramp of Sort-It Squad boots came closer and closer . . .

Delilah grabbed the handle of the wardrobe and flung it open. They were both about to help Pug inside but there was no need. He bounced up; clearly he had the same sort of springs as Granny G.

'We'll come and get you,' whispered Babbatunde, closing the door. 'Don't move.'

At that exact and very inconvenient moment his phone started making lion noises again.

There was no time to turn it off.

Buzz Blingman came round the corner of a huge cupboard followed by the captain of the Sort-It Squad, stamping and swaying and carrying a massive broom.

'Thank goodness you're here, Colonel-Major and Mr Blingman, sir,' said Babbatunde at once. 'We're so scared. We heard a lion and we ran in here. My mother is buying a lot of shoes.'

The lion had stopped roaring and Babbatunde hadn't been able to answer the phone. Now Sofia was going to be really, really mad.

'Only a small lion,' said Delilah. 'But I'm sure it could give a nasty bite.'

'This is exactly what I was afraid of,' yelled Buzz. 'My brother is going to pay for this. Two innocent customers cowering behind furniture . . . If this gets on the internet I will be the laughing stock of the planet . . .'

The two innocent customers tried to look scared. It wasn't difficult. The wardrobe door had not shut completely. Delilah could hear the rattle of a grabber as someone tried to close it from inside.

The captain of the Sort-It Squad was staring at her very hard. He swayed slightly from side to side, brandishing his broom. Then his nose lit up and began to flash on and off.

'CI-VIL-IANS ANSWER QUESTIONS!' he shouted suddenly. 'HAVE CI-VIL-IANS SEEN

SMALL PROTOTYPE ROBOT?'

Other members of the squad had followed him. They were making a sort of traffic jam in the narrow space behind him, stamping on the spot.

Delilah leant against the wardrobe door and it shut with a clunk. There was a faint beep from inside.

'Do NOT bother customers with our problems,' said Buzz very sternly. 'And please reverse your squad, before they stand on someone.' The captain was practically standing on him already.

Buzz quickly covered his ears. The captain gave the order to reverse. It was clear that he had only one volume. Very, very LOUD. Delilah and Babbatunde held on to each other like people in a high wind.

The squad began to back out of the maze, banging into the cupboards and bookcases as they went. The captain saluted and backed after them.

'Now,' said Buzz, pulling his worry beads out of his pocket. 'I am the Owner-in-Chief of this store. Allow me to offer our sincere apologies. We have been having problems with lion noises and piles of pianos this morning. If you will follow me I would like to present you with gift tokens to make up for the inconvenience you have suffered.'

'Thank you,' said Babbatunde, who was looking very tense. 'But I absolutely have to get back to the shoe department at once. I'm supposed to be meeting my mum there and I'm late.'

At that moment his phone started ringing again.

Mr Blingman jumped into a position of alert readiness. 'Don't worry, children,' he said through clenched teeth. 'It's not a *real* lion. It's coming from a loudspeaker hidden somewhere in this department by my brother. He's sneaked over from New York to try and scare off all my customers.'

'I'm sorry, we're sorry,' gabbled Delilah. 'We must go *now*!'

She glanced at the wardrobe where Pug was hiding. Was that a very small beeping she could hear?

'We'll be back,' she said, raising her voice. 'Really soon.'

'I am coming to look for you NOW,' said Babbatunde's phone, sounding very cross indeed.

Babbatunde started coughing to try and drown it out. Not a realistic plan. Even when she was only talking the Songbird of Amania had a formidable voice.

'I'm warning you, you are in *big* trouble. You are grounded for a *week*, from *now*.'

Mr Blingman looked around, frowning at this new danger.

'Don't threaten me, Vinnie,' he said, narrowing his eyes. 'And don't threaten my helicopter either.'

Babbatunde and Delilah were falling over each other's bags and feet.

'Thank you,' shouted Delilah over her shoulder.

They rushed out of the maze, banging into each other, past the captain and the Sort-It Squad, who were staggering about with several pianos, and on, out of the furniture section, and back towards the shoe department.

Three assistants were just getting on to the escalator carrying piles of shoeboxes. Someone was marching out of the shoe department behind them.

'Tunde!' cried Sofia. Everyone who heard her jumped. In fact, all three assistants very nearly demonstrated the terrible dangers of tip bang stairs when they are not approached with care.

13

Back at the House

'He's grounded tomorrow,' said Delilah, coming to the end of telling Granny Grabbers everything that had happened at Blingman's.

Granny Grabbers rolled her headlamps, shrugged some shoulders and beeped sympathetically. She was parked on sheets of newspaper and in the middle of oiling her joints. Despite the paper, quite a lot of oil had found its way on to the kitchen floor.

'Do you really need quite that much?' asked Delilah. Her parents would be coming home from work soon.

'Must be able to move silently,' said Granny Grabbers, who now seemed to be oiling her ear. 'Like owl.'

'Owl?'

'Our native wildlife of woodland. Owl is silent night-time predator. Wings make no noise. Only noise is too whit too whoo. Which owl can switch on and off.'

'We're not going to *fly* to Blingman's to rescue Pug, are we?' Delilah had known Granny Grabbers for long enough to be prepared for anything.

Granny Grabbers' eyes flashed red.

'Exciting but difficult to

organize,' she said after a moment. 'We stick plan. We inform Boy Genie. He can be much big help without leaving Embassy.' Boy Genie was her personal name for Babbatunde. He didn't let anyone else use it. (He had won a lot of chess competitions when he was younger and been called a Boy Genius in the newspaper.)

'But what exactly *is* the plan?'

'Blingman's store open tonight Late-Night Easter Extragander. We travel in grabbmobile in suitable disguise. Boy Genie hack into security cameras. He will be like eye of fly and other insects. Many little screens. Advise on location security guards, exits and things.'

'Oh, goodness,' said Delilah.

'We enter shop in disguise and findy Pug. Then we rescue him.'

'Oh, goodness,' repeated Delilah. 'Oh, goodness me.'

'Grabbmobile, costumes and all-important props at the readies. Note for Mr and Mrs

Smart saying we go Blingman's all clear. Child Unit have tea. Rendezvoo garage eighteen forty-five hours pm o'clock in twenty minutes precisely. Grabbers will telephone Boy Genie and advise hacking procedure.'

'Oh no,' said Delilah. 'Oh no, oh dear . . . Is Sir Isaac coming too?'

'Of course. Sir Isaac is battle-ready.'

'He's what?'

Delilah peered at Sir Isaac. He was sitting on the kitchen table wearing his flying goggles. The whole room – in fact, most of the house – now smelt of Moonlight Mystery.

'What do you mean, battle-ready?'

'In case enemy action result in unforeseen change of plan. Bear is part of back-up plan. Always have back-up plan. Always cleans teeths.'

And Granny Grabbers rattled off back to her secret room.

14

Babbatunde at the Embassy

Meanwhile, Babbatunde was sitting on a ridiculously large and comfortable chair in a ridiculously large and comfortable room on the top floor of the Amanian Embassy. He was miserable.

His father was in a meeting with important people and the Songbird of Amania was still cross and in the bath.

Shoes, tissue paper and shoeboxes littered the floor everywhere he looked.

He sighed deeply at the unfairness of the universe, turned on his laptop and typed

MORSEL and CODE into the search engine by mistake.

'Did you mean *Morse* code?' asked the computer smugly.

Then his mobile started roaring.

'Attention all shipping, good evening and welcome to tonight's mission. Your secret orders,' said a familiar voice, echoing and booming. 'Grabbers here,' it informed him, although this was not necessary. 'Boy Genie turn off television and any other sources of distractification.'

Babbatunde gave a whoop and turned absolutely everything off.

'Except laptop,' added Granny Grabbers.

Babbatunde turned his laptop on again. He couldn't stop grinning. She probably wanted him to look something up for her . . . on the other hand, surely she could look things up just as easily herself, in which case, what . . . ?

'Are you sitting at attention?' said Granny Grabbers.

'Yes,' whispered Babbatunde, hoping very much that Sofia would have an especially long bath.

'Mission Easter Bunny starting in twenty minutes when Grabbers and Child Unit leave Smart house on grabbmobile which motorbike shed. Grabbers will now give steppy-step instructions. Boy Genie will listen with due care and attention.'

Back in her secret

room, Granny Grabbers was wondering if perhaps she'd been a bit over-enthusiastic with the oil. Her voice was beginning to glug a bit. 'Boy Genie glug prepare to hack into security camera system of Blingman's big shiny show-off department shop,' she announced. 'Glug. Grabbers will commence instructions now.'

Babbatunde almost fell out of the ridiculously comfy chair. 'What? What do you mean, hack—'

'Boy Genie glug is much big ready glug fingers over keyboard standby?'

'Oh, yes,' said Babbatunde, who had completely forgotten that he had ever been miserable or bored in his life. 'But, Granny G, this is seriously illegal—'

'In the event of criminal vestigation Grabbers will take the music and face the rap,' said Granny Grabbers. 'Nobody ever arrest robot yet.'

Sometime later, Sofia emerged from the beautiful ensuite bathroom in a floating turquoise gown with a matching scarf around her hair.

'I am going to rehearse,' she said. 'Your father will be back later. Please do not leave this room.'

'I won't,' said Babbatunde.

'I'm sorry if it is boring for you but you must learn always to phone when you have said you will phone and come back when you have said you will come back and not cause your mother any worry. Think about that, please.'

'I will, Mother,' said Babbatunde solemnly, as she closed the door.

His laptop screen had suddenly filled with little televisions. This must be almost as good as sitting in the security guards' office at Blingman's. He could see the front doors, the back door, all sorts of shoppers looking at all sorts of things.

Every part of the shop had been decorated with yellow and gold streamers, little fluffy chicks (the ones in the pet department were real), pyramids of chocolates and bunches of paper daffodils.

More importantly, he could see something deeply strange, that looked very like a garden shed, arriving at the back entrance by the many dustbins. He could just make out two wheels underneath. It lumbered to a halt, lowered itself until it was standing on the ground and then tilted a bit towards the kerb. It had 'Workmen at Work On Gas' painted on the side in shaky letters. Undoubtedly done by grabber.

'Brilliant,' breathed Babbatunde.

The door of the shed opened and someone staggered out wearing face paint and whiskers and dressed as, well, probably a rabbit. The costume was very saggy and baggy, the ears were especially enormous. However, there was no mistaking Delilah. She was carrying Sir Isaac, who was wearing his sunglasses and a pair of very fluffy pink rabbit ears with sparkly bits on them. He had whiskers stuck on his face with sticky tape.

Then the shed started bouncing and rocking about. Someone else seemed to be trying to get out and they were clearly having trouble. Finally the whole thing lifted up at the back and a very barrel-shaped, six-armed Easter Bunny rolled into the road and struggled upright. She was covered in pale-pink fur with visible stitching and buttons. She had a large white rabbit tail, a bit too near her armpits on one side, and pink-lined floppy rabbit ears, which kept folding down over her headlamps.

All three of them were carrying baskets of Easter eggs. Babbatunde suspected that Granny Grabbers' basket was the one the Smarts used for their laundry because he could just make out a sock in there among the eggs. Sir Isaac's basket was tied to his chest.

The six-armed Easter Bunny lifted something out of her basket and held it in front of her headlamps, the only parts of her person that were not covered in fur.

Babbatunde's phone started roaring. He picked it up.

'Grabbers to Mission Control,' said Granny Grabbers, very muffled by the rabbit costume. 'Request information. Describe fifth-floor furniture department. Over.'

Babbatunde scanned all the little screens. He discovered that they were numbered.

'Lots of those big noisy robot-types moving stuff around. They've taken down the slide.

Looks like they're starting on the maze,' he said after a moment. 'Not beautiful like you, Granny G. That massive one with the red nose telling everyone what to do . . .'

At that instant something else caught his eye. It was happening in a different screen, not the furniture department at all.

'Hang on, Granny G . . . I don't believe it, there's a man *climbing in through a window* . . . not in the furniture department, on another floor.'

'Focus furnitures. You see Pug anywhere?'

'No, no . . . not yet. But there's definitely a man climbing in a window . . . I didn't realize they had security cameras in toilets. Well, it's not actually *in* the toilet. He's putting on some sort of costume . . . Granny G, he's dressing up as the Easter Bunny too, just like you and Delilah and Sir Isaac! Well, not *exactly* like you but—'

'Keep eyes on screens,' glugged his mobile. 'Rescue team going in.'

Babbatunde scrolled frantically down until

he found a screen covering the back entrance again. The picture changed from the door itself, with the Staff Only sign, to the dustbins and the grabbmobile and back again. The door was swinging to and fro. The Easter Bunnies had disappeared.

'Thank you, miss control,' said his mobile.

'This is so cool,' muttered Babbatunde, surveying his many changing screens. 'This is absolutely living the dream.'

15

In the Staff Locker Room

In Delilah's opinion they were living the nightmare. She was quite certain that it was against all sorts of laws to drive about in a grabbmobile made out of a motorbike with a shed over it. Even though, as Granny Grabbers kept pointing out, the shed had windows and, in fact, wing mirrors.

Now, adding more crimes to the list, they were entering Blingman's, a place bristling with security guards, under extremely false pretences.

'I'm sure we can be arrested for pretending to

be the Easter Bunny,' she said as they paused inside the Staff Only entrance to tidy their eggs and straighten their ears.

'Easter Bunny is always pretend,' said Granny Grabbers scornfully. 'Follow Grabbers.'

Delilah followed, sick with nerves.

They were in a staffroom, full of lockers. A woman was opening one and hanging her coat inside. She looked up. Her eyes widened. Granny Grabbers was trundling towards her.

'Good evenings, good evenings, we are Easter Buns.'

The woman nodded, staring.

'We go all over shop, givvy out eggy. Ancient symbol. Hope. New life. Rebirth. Chocolate. Very nice,' added the largest Easter Bun rather fiercely, flicking an ear away from her headlamp.

Delilah bobbed beside her, smiling in terror.

'Would you like an egg?' she asked,

holding out her bin.

The woman took a small egg. She seemed to be having trouble taking her eyes off the largest bunny, who was now knotting her troublesome ears over the top of her head using two of her six grabbers.

'Visibility problems,' said the bunny, glugging slightly. 'We wish to deliver eggs to furniture department.'

'Fifth floor,' said the woman, clutching her egg so hard that her thumb went right through it. 'The lift is just through those swing doors, on the left. Or you could use the escalator—'

'NO tip bang stairs, thank you.' The bunny's eyes had turned bright purple. 'Thank you, *no* tip bang stairs, *thanking* you.' She was talking faster and faster. 'Many thanks and a merry Christmas, no tip bang stairs, no, no—'

'Thank you very much,' said Delilah quickly.

She tried to nudge Granny Grabbers, hurt her elbow and squeezed Sir Isaac by mistake.

'E is for egg,' he said, sounding as if he had been having a little doze. Which was, of course, impossible.

16

Alarm in the Lift

They arrived at the swing doors on to the shop floor, which Granny Grabbers hit at some speed, and they shot straight into the very crowded perfume department.

'Lefty turn,' said Granny Grabbers in what might have seemed to her to be a whisper. (What with oil and the furry costume, she wasn't hearing as well as normal.)

Delilah looked round anxiously for the lifts. Oh good, there they were. And oh bad, quite a few people were clustered round the doors waiting to get in. Now they would have to queue. Something Granny Grabbers hated doing.

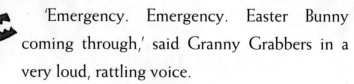

'Emergency. Emergency. Easter Bunny coming through,' said Granny Grabbers in a very loud, rattling voice.

Startled customers backed away in all directions.

'Do please take an egg,' squeaked Delilah, holding out her basket.

The nearest lift arrived. It was on its way up from the basement. The doors hissed open and several customers came out, loaded with bags.

Delilah gave a squeak of horror and ducked down. There was someone else in the lift, waiting for it to go up further. He was tall, beautifully covered from head to foot in silky brown fur; his ears were the right size and were not knotted over his head and he was carrying a huge golden basket of huge golden eggs in one of only two front paws. He was a very official-looking Easter Bunny. He even had a badge with 'Blingman's' written on it.

She tried to stop Granny Grabbers but it was too late. Granny Grabbers barged into the lift and stood right next to him. Delilah followed, staring miserably at the floor.

No doubt some of the other people would have liked to get in the lift too. They certainly moved forwards, cheerful and full of purpose. But Granny Grabbers held up a pink furry grabber, said very loudly, 'Doors squashing,' and pressed the button. The doors began to close, despite the fact that there were only three Easter Bunnies and a bear and therefore plenty of room for at least six more people. A man tried to squeeze himself through the gap, now very narrow, but was pushed firmly back with a single shove of a grabber.

Delilah got a last glimpse of his outraged expression, the doors closed with a clunk and they were off.

'What floor you want?' Granny Grabbers

asked the other Easter Bunny.

Delilah closed her eyes. This was it. The real Blingman's Easter Bunny was going to unmask them. They would be thrown out. And arrested.

But the other Easter Bunny didn't reply to Granny Grabbers and didn't seem interested in getting anyone arrested either. He said nothing and stared straight ahead.

Granny Grabbers rattled some grabbers with annoyance.

'You want button?' She waved at the array of buttons. He still said nothing. She pressed number five.

The lift speeded up and slowed down. It was a very fast lift. They reached the fifth floor and the doors opened.

Delilah hugged Sir Isaac. 'S is for stomach and sick,' he informed the people waiting to get in.

'Easter eggies,' Granny Grabbers told them sternly. 'Take eggy and get out of way.'

Only two of them dared to take an egg. Delilah looked over her shoulder. The official Easter Bunny had already disappeared.

'Granny . . .' she whispered, trying to keep up without banging into anyone. Past the entrance to the shoe department. Past the big display of umbrellas and escalators.

Granny Grabbers beeped with fright.

'Tippy bang,' she said, pointing. 'Child

Unit extreme caution.'

'Oh, are you giving away eggs?' said a woman who seemed to have a whole birthday party of children with her. 'How lovely. Please can we have some?'

Delilah was surrounded.

'Don't snatch,' said the woman. 'Say thank you nicely. Don't push. Don't bite . . .'

'M is for manners,' growled a disgruntled voice.

'That's not a bunny,' said a small boy, poking Sir Isaac in the chest. 'That's just a big old bear with silly rabbit ears. Why's he wearing sunglasses?'

'Now, now . . .' began the woman faintly.

'S is for shut it,' said Sir Isaac.

A few moments later Delilah was scurrying after Granny Grabbers who had driven herself straight into the tape saying No Entry, turned round, reversed and become stuck.

They had arrived.

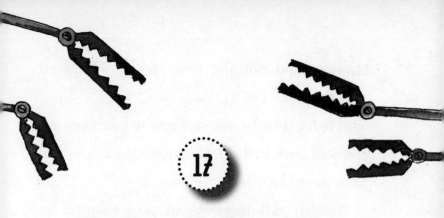

Finding the Wardrobe

While all this had been going on, Babbatunde
had been zooming in and out of one screen after
another. He had found Granny Grabbers and
Delilah when they were getting into the lift. He
had seen them arrive on the fifth floor and
progress with caution past the top of the
escalators. He had also seen the other Easter
Bunny hurry to the pet department. Now that
furry person was hiding behind a display of fish
tanks – he was getting some things out of his
basket and they definitely were not golden eggs.

'So that's why you came in by the toilet

window and not the front door,' whispered Babbatunde.

He had tried to phone Granny Grabbers but she had switched off her ringtone. (It was the Dentists of Doom.)

Finally, getting more and more alarmed, he had seen Dollie and Billie Blingman being photographed in the café eating doughnuts and Buzz Blingman wandering around the store, checking on things and waving his string of worry beads about. He was now walking through the shoe section. It looked as if he wanted to check how things were going in his furniture department.

On the furniture department monitor, Granny Grabbers had at last been untangled. She reached into her basket . . .

Babbatunde's phone started roaring. He snatched it up.

'Come in, Boy Genie,' barked Granny Grabbers. 'Miss Control see Pug?'

'No, not yet but, Granny G, listen, it's very important, I've been trying to call you, the other Easter Bunny, the one I told you about who came in through the toilet window, he's—'

'We seen other bunny,' said Granny Grabbers testily. 'He not news.'

'But he's not real, he's not a real Easter Bunny and—'

'Of course he not real!' Granny Grabbers banged the mobile against the side of her head in frustration.

Babbatunde doubled up, covering his ears. How stressful could a phone conversation get?

At that moment the monitor switched to another camera, deep in the heart of the furniture department. With his head still ringing he shouted, 'I can see the wardrobe! It's rocking! I think Pug's trying to get out! And the place is crawling with Sort-It Squad!'

'Over and outer,' boomed Granny Grabbers. Her headlamps flashed into purple, she dropped her mobile, ran over it, beeped, waved some grabbers and set off.

Delilah picked up the phone, jammed it in her basket and clung on to Granny Grabbers' nearest grabber, trying to slow her down. It was a bit like trying to slow down a tank.

They could hear thuds and bangs and the voices of the Sort-It Squad raised in song. *'Clean is good and grime is BAD! Grime's a crime it makes us MAD!'*

Then they narrowly missed colliding with four squad members who stamped past carrying a grand piano over their heads. The floor shook.

The slide was gone. The very expensive table was just a table again, with a vase standing in the middle of it. The cushion pyramid had all been taken down. Half the maze had already been removed.

The Easter Bunnies sneaked forwards. Towards the long row of cupboards and wardrobes. Granny Grabbers pulled the spare bunny costume that she had made for Pug out from the bottom of her egg basket.

'It's that one,' whispered Delilah. She recognized the wardrobe because there was a carved flower on the door. There was another clue too. Babbatunde had been right: the whole thing was rocking from side to side.

Granny Grabbers beeped something rapidly. The wardrobe stopped rocking. There was a tiny silence. Then it began beeping back. Slowly and quietly at first, then faster and faster and more and more loudly.

'Ssh!' hissed Delilah.

Granny Grabbers beeped something to the wardrobe and it fell silent.

'Pug very happy,' Granny Grabbers told Delilah unnecessarily. Her bunny tail had fallen off. She stuck it on the back of her head.

'Don't you think you should untie your ears?' whispered Delilah.

But there was no more time for personal

grooming. The captain was coming from one direction and yet more Sort-Its were coming from the other, carrying carpets.

'Child Unit distract. Grabbers will release Pug and assist into disguise,' said Granny Grabbers.

She rolled up to the wardrobe and thumped the lock with three grabbers at once.

The door swung open.

Pug fell out.

There was a tremendous explosion of beeps and grabbers. Two pairs of headlamps, one large and one small, flashed red, pink, blue and back to red again. Clutching each other in all six grabbers, Pug and Granny Grabbers spun around like a fairground ride, almost knocking Delilah over.

She jumped about, trying to stop them, swatting at Granny Grabbers.

'Quick! Stop! Mr Blingman's coming with lots of people!'

Mr Blingman was indeed coming, together with the captain, the head of security and Miss Treen.

With impressive speed, Granny Grabbers picked up Pug, put him back into the wardrobe and slammed it shut.

18

Buying the Wardrobe

'The Sort-It Squad have done an excellent job in here. Everything – well, almost everything – is back in its right position, sir,' said Miss Treen, pausing alarmingly near the wardrobe.

Buzz Blingman nodded vigorously, swinging his worry beads.

'Very good, very good, very good . . .'

'Unfortunately we've still not found the person or persons responsible for the lion noises, sir,' said the head of security.

'It's not *persons*, it's my brother Vinnie,' said Buzz. 'And I'm sure he's in the store *as we speak.*

He's determined to ruin my Easter Extravaganza—' He stopped.

He had finally noticed Granny Grabbers and Delilah. So had everyone else. All eyes were upon them.

'Good evenings, hello, welcomes to Easter. Springtime, lambykins and happy, happy bunny eggs,' said Granny Grabbers.

Delilah held out her basket, blushing. Out of the corner of her eye she saw the wardrobe rock, very slightly, from side to side.

'You likee eggy?' demanded Granny Grabbers.

Buzz Blingman frowned. He narrowed his eyes.

'Who are you, exactly?' he asked.

'Easter Buns,' said Granny Grabbers.

There was a very small, anxious beep from inside the wardrobe. The captain of the Sort-It Squad stared at it. His nose lit up.

'I didn't know we had any Easter Buns, I

mean Bunnies,' said Buzz.

'We're code 10,' said Delilah quickly. 'We're the bunnies no one knows they don't know about. To – to surprise and, um, delight the customers.'

Her mouth was dry. She felt as if her legs were going to give way.

Suddenly the captain of the Sort-It Squad lurched forwards with his massive arms outstretched and started rattling the handle of the wardrobe door and then thumping on it with his fist.

Delilah screamed. Granny Grabbers' eyes flashed bright green. She began to roll towards him . . .

'What on earth are you doing?' yelled Mr Blingman. 'This is a top-of-the-range, hand-carved mahogany wardrobe worth three thousand pounds!'

'SIR, MR BLINGMAN, SIR! BEEPING NOISE COMING FROM IN HERE, SIR!

PROTOTYPE MAKES BEEPS. SIR!'

Mr Blingman took his hands away from his ears. 'Can't we just unlock it?'

'SIR, MR BLINGMAN, SIR! PROTOTYPE IS HOLDING SHUT FROM THE INSIDE. SIR!'

The captain picked up the wardrobe and began shaking it like a ketchup bottle.

'PUT IT DOWN!' cried Mr Blingman.

'Put down or I pull off your head, Rudolf,' hissed Granny Grabbers, very scarily, into the captain's ear.

The captain put down the wardrobe. It made a worried beeping sound. Granny Grabbers quickly beeped too. No doubt some words of reassurance.

'SIR, MR BLING—'

'Everyone be quiet!' said Buzz Blingman fiercely.

Everyone was quiet. Even the captain, even though it was clear that he thought it was all very unfair.

Silence.

More silence.

Then Granny Grabbers held out her basket and lowered her headlamp lids demurely.

'Chocolates are eggies,' she said. 'Misunderstandment. Your esteemed soldier cleaner robot thought my natural beep emerge wardrobe. But it emerge me.' She beeped again. The wardrobe said nothing.

Delilah hugged Sir Isaac tightly.

'B is for Blingman's, best buys and bargains,' said Sir Isaac loudly.

Buzz Blingman's face cracked into a smile.

'Easy mistake, Captain, thinking you heard the noise coming from inside the wardrobe . . . no harm done. Excellent bear. I mean rabbit.'

The captain of the Sort-It Squad was still leaning towards the wardrobe and stomping gently on the spot. He obviously wasn't programmed to understand when someone was holding on to him from behind. In this case Granny Grabbers, who had extended a grabber discreetly and latched on to his dustpan attachment.

'We would like buy this wardyrobe,' she said, flicking her ears over the back of her head yet again. 'You take creddy card?'

Mr Blingman ducked as she waved a number of cards in his face.

Delilah spotted her own library card and Mr Smart's membership of the Dinky Wrinkles Tanning Studios among them.

'Pick a card, any card,' said Granny Grabbers cheerfully.

'We're always delighted to make a sale,' began Mr Blingman, selecting a proper credit card and putting the others back in an outstretched grabber. 'Delivery is free, of course, for luxury items like this.'

'We carry home now,' said Granny Grabbers.

Delilah tried to pull a face at her, but her

whiskers got in the way.

'Would you like it gift-wrapped?' asked Miss Treen. 'I'll go and fetch some wrapping paper . . . a lot of wrapping paper . . . and several metres of, er, ribbon.' She hurried away.

19

Spiders

Everything was looking good. Then, suddenly, the head of security started to ring and buzz alarmingly, pulled three flashing mobile phones out of different pockets and gabbled, 'Incoming! Emergency!'

'What emergency? It's my brother, isn't it?'

'Spiders loose throughout the store, sir.'

Mr Blingman leapt into a BashaNosa Defence Posture. As if he was trying to wave to a friend and stand on one leg at the same time.

Delilah's own phone, the one that sounded like violent washing-up, began to make crashing

and splashing noises in her basket.

Now there were shouts from the entrance of the furniture department; the head of security was speaking rapidly into all his phones; Mr Blingman was jumping up and down, pointing at the floor.

A large, black tarantula-type spider was scuttling towards them over a pile of expensive rugs.

'It's the other Easter Bunny,' crackled Babbatunde's voice in Delilah's ear. 'He's got all these spiders. He's been creeping about letting them go. They're . . . CRACKLE . . . crackle . . . *robotic*. He's climbing out of the same window he came in by—'

'Stand back! Remain calm! Everything's under control!' shouted Mr Blingman, hopping from one foot to another, jumping out of the way of the captain of the Sort-It Squad, who had finally given up on the wardrobe and was trying to stamp on the nearest spider.

The spiders, and there were now a lot of them, were huge and hairy with lots of twinkling eyes on the front. They were much too quick for anyone to stamp on.

One ran towards Delilah, who couldn't help screaming, and then it seemed to aim towards Mr Blingman, waving its front legs and whirring.

'A is for arachnid!' cried Sir Isaac.

'I know it's you, Vinnie,' Mr Blingman told it from on top of the back of a sofa. 'You know I can't stand spiders. I'm going to get you for this, you evil, plotting—'

'HALT, VINNIE!' commanded the captain of the Sort-It Squad.

The spider waved some legs and ran off. He chased after it, knocking over a grandfather clock.

Only Granny Grabbers remained calm. As more spiders and escaping customers and security men came scuttling and running and striding into the furniture department she

whispered to Delilah, 'We leave wardrobe. Take Pug. Fire exit. Over there.'

Delilah nodded. A spider had just run over her foot.

'Fire exit is not tip bang stairs?'

Delilah shook her head.

'Then back door and into grabbmobile.'

Delilah nodded again.

Once more, all would quite possibly have been well. Granny Grabbers trundled through the chaos and opened the wardrobe door.

Pug bounced out, eyes flashing, grabbers waving and all three of them turned towards the fire exit.

Then – horrors.

Billie and Dollie Blingman came hurtling up to Buzz, out of breath and wildly excited. As soon as they reached him (still perched on the sofa) they both started talking at the same time.

'There's spiders everywhere! Dad, can we catch one and take it home? Please, Dad, please!'

Then they saw Pug. The escape plan hadn't quite worked yet …

Pug had seen the captain in the distance and was refusing to move.

'Is that the robot who built the slide and moved all the pianos?' cried Billie. 'I want him for my birthday!'

'ARREST PROTOTYPE!' bellowed the

captain of the Sort-It Squad. 'WE FIGHT GRIME ALL THE TIME!'

Granny Grabbers was picking spiders off her person and throwing them in all directions without looking. One bounced off the captain's head.

'PROTOTYPE, DO SIX HUNDRED PRESS-UPS!' he yelled, as another spider hit him on the nose.

Security men were shooing people back the way they had come. A soothing voice over the loudspeakers was trying to invite customers to visit the chocolate department.

'We buy robot,' gurgled Granny Grabbers, once more at this critical moment troubled by oil. She waved Mr Smart's Bankus Maximus card. 'You namey price?'

Mr Blingman jumped bravely down from the back of the sofa. He couldn't resist the chance of doing business.

'We can't let it go for less than a thousand

pounds,' he said quickly. 'It's unique.' He looked from Granny Grabbers to Pug and back again. 'Almost.'

'Done,' said Granny Grabbers.

'Traffic wardens are trying to wheel-clamp the shed,' said Babbatunde in Delilah's ear. 'But they don't seem to be able to find the wheels.'

'But *I* want the robot,' said Dollie Blingman, shaking her unbelievably shiny curls. 'I want to dress it up to match my clothes. Godawfulla Gobblethwaite has a little dog. She takes him everywhere. Why should Billie have the robot? That's not fair.'

'I saw him first!' yelled Billie, getting hold of Dollie by the hair. 'And he doesn't want to dress up! He's a boy!'

'Get off me!' screamed Dollie, grabbing *his* hair and pulling it most dreadfully.

'Twins!' cried Buzz. He threw a spider so violently that it hit the captain and exploded. 'Let go of each other NOW! Stop this at once.

You can *share* the robot. We'll decide what to do when we get home—'

'I don't want share him!' yelled Billie and Dollie at the same time.

'And I don't know what your mother's going to say if you mess up your hair.'

'SO WHAT? I wish I didn't have hair!' Billie informed the world from the floor. 'And it's my robot and I'm not sharing it!'

Buzz groaned and wiped his forehead with his hand. 'I'm very sorry, Mr Smart,' he said to Granny Grabbers, looking sadly at the Bankus Maximus card before he handed it back. 'But my kids do seem very keen . . .' He stepped over the twins and returned to the back of the sofa. 'You see, my wife doesn't let them have pets. Not actual animals, and the robot would be perfect.'

Delilah could see Granny Grabbers clenching her grabbers one by one. It looked as if they were going to have to leave without Pug.

Things couldn't get any worse. Then they did.

'I want that talking rabbit thing instead,' said Dollie suddenly, pointing at Sir Isaac.

Billie let go of her. She let go of him. They both stood up.

'Billie can have the robot. I can dress the rabbit thing up instead. She's cuter.'

'He's a he,' said Delilah. 'And he's a bear, actually. He's just dressed as a rabbit. And he's not for sale.'

'That's cool with me,' said Billie. 'You can keep her. Bears are girly. Dad, if Dollie's having the bear I want the robot all to myself, OK?'

'The bear isn't for sale!' said Delilah in a loud voice. She was hugging Sir Isaac very tightly. He started to cough. Then he said, in a hopeful, croaky voice, 'E is for exit.'

'Isn't she sweet,' said Dollie.

'*He* is NOT sweet,' shouted Delilah. 'And NO WAY is *he* for SALE.'

Thank goodness Granny Grabbers was

there. Thank goodness she would never, ever let anyone take Sir Isaac away.

Then something unbelievable, unthinkable and terrible happened.

'Of course you have bear,' said Granny Grabbers, her headlamps all sugar sweet pink. 'You are most big welcome to bear.'

She hissed at Delilah, 'Bulletin later explain.' Then she simply lifted Sir Isaac out of Delilah's arms and gave him to Dollie.

'And a happy birthday to you twinners,' added Granny Grabbers grandly, 'from the Easter Bunners.'

Delilah couldn't move. She couldn't speak.

She watched with her mouth open as Dollie and Billie Blingman took charge of Pug and Sir Isaac.

Buzz climbed back on to the sofa. 'Well, how generous, thank you, but surely—' he began. But no one heard whatever he was going to say because Granny Grabbers fired off a whole paragraph of beeps. Pug beeped sadly back.

'We go now,' said Granny Grabbers to Delilah.

The head of security had just pushed his way through the crowds back to Buzz. He climbed on to the back of the sofa to talk to him.

'Progress report, sir.'

'Have you found my brother?'

'We have witnesses who say they saw someone in an Easter Bunny costume getting spiders out of their egg basket and releasing them in the food hall, sir.'

Mr Blingman narrowed his eyes, whistled through his teeth and wrinkled his nose.

'Are you telling me that my fiendish brother has disguised himself as a round robot with six arms disguised as a pink rabbit?'

'With respect, Mr Blingman, sir, the rabbit witnesses saw was a two-armed type of rabbit, sir. Tall with brown fur and smelling slightly of aftershave, sir.'

'That's him, all right,' said Buzz. 'That's my brother Vinnie.'

He looked around him at the customers, many of them running about and climbing on to furniture themselves. The furniture department was full of screams and yells and scuttling spiders. No doubt the whole store was the same.

'He never leaves me alone,' said Buzz very quietly. Only one person heard him. That was Granny Grabbers, with her excellent robotic auditory detector system. She swivelled her head to look back at him. Then she bustled Delilah through the door of the fire escape.

And Babbatunde just had enough time to watch them climbing safely back into the grabbmobile before Sofia the Songbird of Amania came back from rehearsals and he had to turn off the laptop and look bored.

20

Tension in the Grabbmobile

All was not well in the grabbmobile. Granny Grabbers adjusted her own helmet. Then she adjusted Delilah's. She bounced up on to the seat of Mr Smart's expensive motorbike and extended two grabbers to the places where Mr Smart would have put his feet.

She lowered her goggles. Then, sensing that all was not quite right, she swivelled her head to look at Delilah. Delilah was not on the bike. She was still standing beside it. She was holding Sir Isaac Newton's helmet and glaring.

'Child Unit attention, all hurry,' said Granny

Grabbers. 'Escape scheduled for now at once.'

'How could you,' whispered Delilah in tones most terrible. 'How could you *give* him to that horrible, that, that, *girl* . . . I'm not going *anywhere* . . . I . . . am . . . not . . . moving . . . I will never, *ever* forgive you for as long as I live, *ever* . . .'

Granny Grabbers started waving all her grabbers.

'Child Unit must believe. Sir Isaac not given away. No, no negative no. Sir Isaac daring and brave. He agent behind enemy lines. He send back vital information to the head mission base quarters.'

Delilah stared at her in amazement.

Then they both thought they heard voices muttering outside the grabbmobile. Or maybe even on top of it.

Delilah jumped on to the back seat. Granny Grabbers revved the engine. And they were off. Much to the surprise of the two pigeons who had been cooing on the roof.

21

Contact with Sir Isaac

They were home. The house was quiet. Except for the sounds of Mr and Mrs Smart practising their arm-wrestling in the living room again.

Delilah and Granny Grabbers were in the private room under the stairs.

Delilah could not remember ever seeing it packed with so many things. Granny Grabbers' six-armed magic costume was here, including the hat, and several packs of cards. Her laptop was open at a website selling equipment for magicians. Normally Delilah would have wanted to see this. Not tonight.

She sat down on the workbench.

'I know you said we must keep calm and everything will be all right, but I don't see how—'

'Soothing palaver light,' said Granny Grabbers, switching on her violently lime-green lava lamp. 'Child Unit like hear track from Dentists of Doom?'

Granny Grabbers found the Dentists relaxing. It was not the word Delilah would have used.

She shook her head.

'Child Unit must go very soon bed. But first, latest from newsroom. Sir Isaac in constant audio and visual contact,' said Granny Grabbers. 'He spy in enemy camp.'

'Yeah, you said that, but I don't see how—'

'Behold.'

Granny Grabbers' headlamps flashed red with excitement. She pressed something on her laptop keyboard and the magicians' supplies site disappeared.

Delilah watched, very puzzled, as a dim-lit picture appeared. Everything seemed to be at an angle. She screwed up her eyes and put her head on one side.

She could just about make out a door, slightly open. There was a pink rug on the floor and what looked like a television on the wall . . .

She looked at Granny Grabbers, who pointed a grabber at her auditory detector and then back to the screen.

Delilah realized that she could hear someone breathing in there. Whoever they were, it sounded as if they were asleep.

'Sir Isaac has nosecam,' whispered Granny Grabbers. 'Microphonage in paw.'

'Nosecam?' whispered Delilah. 'A camera in his nose?'

Granny Grabbers nodded. 'New addition,' she said. 'He provide continuous update. For example. Current update is he is located bedroom. Girl Blingman asleep. Child Unit should be asleep too. Children need love, sleep, fruit, vegetables, chocolate cake. Rendezvoo kitchen eight a.m. hours o'clock tomorrow. Always cleans teeth.'

Delilah hugged her.

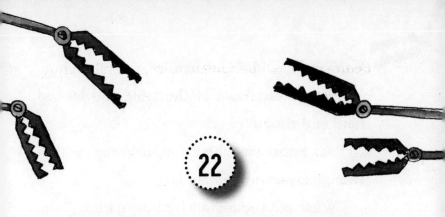

22

Muffins in the Morning

Delilah did not sleep well. It was very lonely without Sir Isaac.

She was up early, just in time to see her parents coming back from their run (they were in training for the Big Brains Institute Extra-Long Marathon). Mr Smart had made some experimental muffins, which he was planning to enter in the Big Brains Institute Muffin-Making Competition.

'Try some and tell me what you think,' he said to Delilah before she had time to sneak away with the delicious muesli Granny

Grabbers had made for her.

Delilah sat down at the table and looked hard at the muffin.

Mrs Smart was there too, chewing, with a strange expression on her face.

'What are these crunchy bits, darling?' she asked after a moment. 'They really are very, very . . . hard. In fact, I think something has happened to my tooth.'

'Charcoal,' said Mr Smart. 'Really good for the digestion.'

Delilah started coughing.

'*Charcoal,*' said Mrs Smart.

'Yes, and these are also *vitamin-enriched* muffins,' said Mr Smart. 'The white bits are pieces of vitamin tablet. It's my own recipe, of course. Brilliant, don't you think?'

'I'm just going to take my muffin into the garden,' said Delilah quietly. 'It's such a lovely morning.'

She could see Granny Grabbers through the

window, hanging washing on the line. It was wild and windy out there. Granny Grabbers was fighting with a sheet and the sheet was winning.

Delilah crept towards the door into the utility room.

'Charcoal and bits of vitamin tablet,' said Mrs Smart in a menacing voice. 'No wonder the bread-making machine was making such a terrible noise before it broke this morning. It sounded as if it was trying to eat a bone.'

'Bone would have been good too, for the calcium,' said Mr Smart. 'But to win this competition I've got to do something really different. That's why I decided to add the chilli powder. For the unexpected kick.'

Delilah was in the utility room. The last thing she heard was Mrs Smart saying a lot of very loud things about giving someone an unexpected kick herself and did Mr Smart realize how much it was going to cost to fix the crown back on her tooth.

'Child Unit has slept well, shower, clean clothes, healthy breakfast?' asked Granny Grabbers when Delilah had rescued her from the sheets and towels and things and put the washing line back up again.

'Please can we have a look through Sir Isaac's nosecam,' said Delilah. She had not slept well: she had slept badly because she was worrying about Sir Isaac and Pug. In fact, she hadn't done any of the things on Granny Grabbers' list at all.

Granny Grabbers peered at her. Then she rummaged around in the bag of clothes pegs slung around her middle and produced something wrapped in greaseproof paper.

'Muffin,' she said.

'Oh, no,' said Delilah.

'Grabbermade, during night,' said Granny Grabbers, 'containing chocolate chippings and banana.'

Delilah took the muffin and had a bite immediately.

'And now, over to Grabbers' private room for our next broadcast. The world according to bear,' said Granny Grabbers.

23

Emergency Response Mode

Delilah peered at the screen of Granny Grabbers' laptop. Not much had changed, except it was daylight. It looked as if Sir Isaac was still in Dollie Blingman's bedroom.

'I think you should have a pink dress. Grey fur is a bit boring,' said a voice. Two hands loomed bigger and bigger and disappeared. The picture swung around, taking in bits of pink ceiling and a fluffy lightshade and then there was a wall. And a mirror on it. A big mirror. And wonderfully, marvellously, there *in* the mirror was Sir Isaac Newton. And, much less wonderfully, there was Dollie Blingman, holding him up so that he could see himself.

Delilah nearly screamed with excitement, relief and horror.

'Obviously I look lovely in this dress,' said Dollie. 'And yours is just the same. Except smaller. Isn't that just the cutest thing? I bet Godawfulla Gobblethwaite has never seen a bear like you.'

The terrible truth was that Sir Isaac Newton had been brushed and combed, and was wearing *lipstick* and a flouncy pink and gold dress.

'Godawfulla is coming to our birthday party on Saturday,' said Dollie. 'She always has everything first. But I'm going to show her this time.'

'E is for egg,' said Sir Isaac doubtfully. He was still wearing his glasses.

Delilah saw Dollie's pretty features rearrange themselves into a frown.

'I hope that's not all you can say,' she said.

'I'm sure you said some other things in the shop.'

'E is for embarrassment,' said Sir Isaac, who was still facing the mirror.

Dollie gave a squeal of surprise.

Back in Granny Grabbers' private room, Delilah grinned.

'Hey, Billie, this bear is so cool,' shouted Dollie. 'Come and squeeze her middle and see what she says.'

There was a reply, too distant for the audience in the private room to hear, then the crash of a door being flung open and Billie Blingman arrived in the picture wearing a ninja outfit and carrying something that looked horribly like Mr Smart's electric razor.

In fact, Delilah was sure that it *was* an electric razor. The clue was that Billie Blingman appeared to have shaved off almost all of his own hair.

'Billie, you're bald. Mum'll go, like, totally mad,' said Dollie.

'Nah, she won't. It's to go with this costume for the party. And it's not bald. It's just very, very short.' He was prodding at Sir Isaac.

'Can't believe you've stuck him in a dress,' he said. 'It looks yucky. Really, really, yucky.'

For a moment Delilah agreed with him. Then she suddenly really, really didn't.

'Let's shave his fur. We can make a shape like a skull and crossbones. We could shave a skull and crossbones on to his chest!'

'But she's not a he, she's a girl! And I don't want her to have a skull and crossbones anywhere.'

Delilah briefly agreed with Dollie. Except about Sir Isaac being a girl, of course.

'Oh, don't be so bo-oring. No one'll see. It'll be under his silly dress—'

'*Her* dress.'

'Whatever. Hold him still, let me take the dress off—'

'No!' yelled Dollie. And Delilah.

The twins started to fight over Sir Isaac, pulling him backwards and forwards, lurching in and out of view in the mirror, sending pictures of armpits and glimpses of the floor . . .

Delilah screamed all the rude words she had ever heard.

Billie's face suddenly filled the screen – then *he* screamed.

And Sir Isaac's voice rang out, much louder and deeper than Delilah had ever heard it before: 'U is for unhand me, sir, you dastardly villain. I warn you. My friends are many and will stop at nothing to obtain my release.'

Sir Isaac was suddenly facing the mirror again but now seemed to be standing on his head on the floor. Dollie and Billie had stopped fighting. Billie was rubbing his arm. They both had their mouths open. So did Delilah.

'I must request that you take a step backwards,' intoned Sir Isaac from the carpet. 'Your breath bears the regrettable stench of poor dental hygiene. Always cleans teeth.'

'That bear gave me an electric shock,' said Billie. 'He's armed.'

Dollie picked up Sir Isaac. Delilah and Granny Grabbers had a perfect view of Billie jumping backwards.

'She's a she,' said Dollie. 'She likes to be called Esmeralda.'

'Sure,' he said quickly. 'If he, I mean she, wants to be called Esmeralda that's fine with me. I don't think he, I mean she, wants to have a skull and crossbones on him, I mean her, after all.'

'No, she doesn't,' said Dollie.

'I've got the robot,' said Billie. 'It's a million times better. I'm going to paint a skull and crossbones on him. Or maybe a severed head.'

He went out of sight and there was the sound of the door closing.

'That was very clever,' said Dollie.

'E is for egg,' said Sir Isaac.

In the private room, Delilah gave Granny Grabbers a very hard stare.

'Emergency response mode,' said Granny Grabbers serenely. 'Big much success.'

24

Pug the Pirate

'Now,' said Granny Grabbers, 'we plan next movies.'

Delilah's eyes widened. Was Sir Isaac's nosecam going on WhoseTube?

'Do you mean our next move?' she said.

'Yes, yes. We insert into birthday party.'

'We insert what into it?'

'Us. And Boy Genie. In disguises.'

'Not Easter Bunnies again?'

Granny Grabbers rolled her headlamps and shook her head.

'Birthday party is big hoo-ha. We insert as

children's entertaining, we—'

'Oh, look!' Delilah pointed at the screen. The picture bounced up and down. It looked as if Sir Isaac was being carried downstairs. Now he was arriving in a big hallway with a black and white floor, like a shiny chessboard. A woman's face swerved into view. Mrs Blingman.

'Oh, Dollie darling, you have dressed up nicely. And your pretty bear too. She will look so sweet on the photographs . . .'

'*He*,' said Delilah.

'BILLIE!' yelled Mrs Blingman. 'WE'RE WAITING!'

A woman went past in the background wearing a maid's uniform and carrying a vacuum cleaner. Everything tilted a bit. Then there was a clunk, like the doors of a lift opening, and Billie appeared at the side of the picture.

'How many times have I told you to use the stairs? The lift is not a toy, and—'

Mrs Blingman stopped talking. She stared at

Billie. She had suddenly forgotten all about the lift right in the middle of ranting about it.

She took several deep breaths . . .

'Billie Blingman, what . . . have . . . you . . . done . . . to . . . your hair?'

'It's just very short, Mum,' said Billie. 'It's to go with my costume for the party.'

'Very short! Very short! There's none of it left! You do realize that we have the photographer from Cutie Curl Hair Products coming here *now*, in about five minutes, especially to take your pictures? They've paid me a lot of money. And they are expecting two cute kids with cute curly hair. You and your sister are famous for being cute and having curly hair. *Yadda Yadda* magazine has paid for exclusive rights to your birthday party because you are so cute and have such curly hair!'

'I hate being cute,' muttered Billie.

Delilah and Granny Grabbers both pointed at the screen at the same moment. Pug had just rolled out of the lift and into the hall. He shook hand to grabber with the maid and she patted him on the head. He was wearing a pirate costume with an eyepatch over one headlamp, a skull and crossbones painted on his front and a little plastic monkey on his head.

'Well, we'll just have to see if they'll do the photo-shoot without you,' continued Mrs Blingman. 'Why can't you be more like Dollie? Look how prettily she has dressed her bear. What have you called her, Dollie?'

'Esmeralda,' said Dollie.

Delilah put her head in her hands.

'E is for egg,' said Esmeralda in sinister tones.

'I'll tidy your hair and then you come into the reception room and get ready for the photographer, Dollie,' said Mrs Blingman. 'She's from *Yadda Yadda* magazine, you know, the people who will be photographing your birthday party. And you, Billie, go upstairs, *not* the lift, the *stairs*, and get a hat. Do you hear me?'

The doorbell rang at that moment. The maid opened it and a man came in carrying cameras and lighting equipment.

Dollie must have picked Sir Isaac up because the scene slipped sideways. Then everything was moving. Then it stayed still again while Mrs Blingman combed Dollie's hair.

Granny Grabbers and Delilah had a last glimpse of Billie and Pug. Pug had somehow got one of his grabbers stuck in the letterbox on the front door. He was rattling it about trying to get it back out again. First the eyepatch fell off. Then the monkey.

The maid very kindly retrieved the monkey.

'Your robot is very sweet,' she said to Billie.

'He's not meant to be sweet,' said Billie. 'He's meant to be scary.'

And much to the horror of the maid and the audience in the secret room, he kicked Pug. He didn't hurt him, of course, but he did hurt his foot. Quite a lot, in fact.

Pug beeped softly and his headlamps flashed green.

Billie, who was hopping on one foot, hopped backwards.

Pug beeped faster and faster.

Granny Grabbers began to chortle (which sounded a bit like water going down a plughole).

Then Sir Isaac's nosecam left the hall behind as Dollie carried him away through a doorway and into a room full of cream-coloured furniture.

Pug's beeps faded into the background. But not before Granny Grabbers had upgraded from the plughole noise to her proper laugh, which sounded like a pneumatic drill.

'Why are you laughing?' cried Delilah with her hands over her ears.

'Pug speak Morsel,' said Granny Grabbers with difficulty. 'He very rude. He say, he say –' she burst into more drilling noises '– he call

Billie a . . .' She exploded with drilling noises, plughole noises and a sound like the starter motor on a car. 'He say Billie should—'

'Wait a minute,' shouted Delilah. 'Are you telling me that all this time, whenever you beep, you've been saying things in Morsel, I mean Morse?'

Granny Grabbers went suddenly quiet.

Then she turned off the laptop.

'We plan next operation,' she said sternly. 'Operation Now You Are Seeing It, Now You Are Not Seeing It Any More.'

'Do you mean Now You See It, Now You Don't?' said Delilah.

Granny Grabbers rattled her headlamp lids.

'Express delivery by post,' she said. 'Madame Amazeyoo and her Amazing Magic Show. Spectacular Feet for all the Family.'

'Oh dear,' said Delilah.

25

Summoning Babbatunde

Babbatunde was pacing about in the ridiculously comfortable suite in the Amanian Embassy. He was longing to speak to Delilah and find out what was happening.

His parents had just set off downstairs to be interviewed for a TV station. What with his father being the President of Amania and his mother the Songbird, they had to do quite a lot of interviews.

He counted to ten, in case his mother came back to change her outfit. This had happened several times already and there were bits of rejected outfits scattered all over the room.

Then he reached for the phone and it started to ring before he had time to dial. A moment later he was holding it at arm's length. Granny Grabbers was on the other end.

'Welcome to world of Magic and Mystery. You come Smart house now for rehearsals. Performance tomorrow afternoon.'

'What are you talking about?' asked Babbatunde. 'Rehearsals for what?'

'You dis-grounded? You free exit embassy? You bring big car and Mr Adeleye?'

'Yes, but—'

'You wish be daring assistant to Madame Amazeyoo and her Magic Show?'

'Yes, of course.' Babbatunde pictured himself in a billowing cape and a top hat. There would probably be a moustache too.

'What's this all about, Granny G?'

But he wasn't going to find out just yet. He heard a scuffle at the other end of the line and Delilah's voice shouted, 'Babbatunde, put the TV news on now!'

He fell over some furniture and turned on the television. Just in time to see Buzz Blingman standing on the steps of his store with the head of security beside him.

'I would like to assure everyone that Blingman's will open today for business as usual,' said Mr Blingman into a forest of microphones held up by the journalists of the world.

'And do you have any information yet about where the spiders came from?'

'Yes, I have a very good idea where the *mechanical, robotic* spiders came from and who released them in our store,' said Mr Blingman. He looked straight into the camera. 'He knows I know. And I can tell him now; one day, somehow, things won't go the way he's planned.'

The picture changed to a newsreader back in the studio.

'Mr Buzz Blingman,' she said. 'Clearly upset

but in fighting mood there after the Late-Night Easter Extravaganza at his new store was ruined by robot spiders. There have been no arrests, although witnesses report seeing a, a . . .' She peered at her autocue. 'A *garden shed with blue and yellow curtains* behaving strangely in the area.'

26

Mr Adeleye

Mr Adeleye drove Babbatunde to the Smarts' house in the diplomatic car.

It was, of course, a very large, luxurious car with various special features. One was the satnav. It was shaped like a small barrel and looked like a biscuit tin (because it had been). There was a hole cut in the side where the screen had been fitted, and various wires and aerials sticking out of the top. As Mr Adeleye pulled up smoothly, and almost silently, at the Smarts' gate, the satnav said in a very familiar voice, 'Big much brakes. You there now. Dried fruit make healthy snack.'

This, of course, was the satnav that Granny Grabbers had made for Mr Adeleye. He turned it on even when he knew the way, just because he liked it so much.

'Do you think Granny G would like any more shopping doing?' said Mr Adeleye.

He and Babbatunde both looked at the house. There was a bang and a flash of purple light in the kitchen. Green smoke drifted out of the window.

'Difficult to say,' said Babbatunde.

Next door's cat, Hercules, wandered out of the utility room carrying a string of red and white spotted sausages.

'But she did ask me to ask you if you might be free to take us somewhere tomorrow afternoon, if that would be possible,' added Babbatunde.

There was another bang from the kitchen.

'I would be delighted,' said Mr Adeleye, grinning.

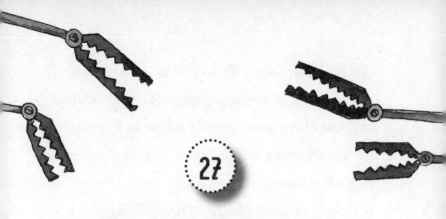

27

The Plan Explained

Mr and Mrs Smart were still at work at the Big Brains Institute and would not be back until late. This was a good thing because the ground floor of the house was now taken up by magic equipment (the living room), special magic effects (the kitchen), actual magic trick rehearsals (the hall) and empty boxes and packaging materials (everywhere).

Dr Doomy, of course, no longer lived in the shed because it had been made into a grabbmobile. He was sitting in the open doorway of his cage, in the kitchen, nibbling a bit of Brain Food Biscuit and watching with interest as Granny Grabbers and Delilah searched for their string of magic sausages.

'Guaranteed hilarious,' said Granny Grabbers scornfully, reading from the empty packet. 'Your family and friends gaspy amazement when string sausage turn into bunch balloons. Then more surprise! Balloon burstment shower little stars.'

There was a bang outside. Delilah, Granny Grabbers and Dr Doomy looked out of the window and saw Hercules the cat leap out of the bushes in a cloud of smoke and silver stars, just as Babbatunde was coming up the path to the front door.

Hercules shot across the grass, trailing the last guaranteed hilarious sausage. Then there was an especially loud bang and a whizzing noise as he jumped on to the wall, sending more stars and some worried birds into the sky.

'Sausages used up,' said Granny Grabbers.

She opened another package, misread the instructions and accidentally set off an indoor firework called sunset volcano and burnt a hole in the carpet.

Delilah hurried to the front door and immediately began to tell Babbatunde everything that had happened and all about Sir Isaac and his secret-agent nosecam.

'We're going to go to the Blingman twins' birthday party. You know how Granny G has had a bit of a craze for learning magic tricks recently? Well, we're going to be children's entertainers,' she told him.

'I didn't know that she could actually *do* any magic,' said Babbatunde.

'We can't do the magic yet, we're going to learn it today. And then we're going to rescue Sir Isaac and Pug by doing a magic trick called The Lady Vanishes. Granny G ordered this cupboard. By special delivery. But it hasn't arrived yet.'

'What hasn't?' asked Babbatunde, stepping over a pile of costumes.

'I just told you. The cupboard. It's called a Vanishing Cupboard. It's a brilliant trick cupboard with a secret compartment. We'll pick Sir Isaac and Pug out of the audience. They'll get in the cupboard and we'll close the door and say abracadabra. Then we'll open the door and they'll have vanished. They'll be hidden in the secret compartment. Then we'll escape.' Delilah was speaking very fast.

Babbatunde stopped stepping over things. He frowned. 'We'll escape. Just like that?'

She nodded. 'We'll set off a lot of indoor fireworks as a diversion. And we'll escape while it's going on.'

He was still frowning. 'That's assuming we get into the party in the first place.'

Delilah nodded again. 'It's got to work,' she whispered, looking as if she was going to cry. 'Because the twins are going back to New York tomorrow. We saw them talking about it on the nosecam. And they'll take Pug and Sir Isaac with them.'

Granny Grabbers came sailing out of the living room, her silver and purple magician's coat swirling around her.

'Continuous broadcast from nosecam on computer screen in private room under the stairs,' she informed Babbatunde. 'Party garden Blingman house tomorrow afternoon. Cupcakes in the Marshy. Very pretty.'

Babbatunde and Delilah stared at her.

'In the marquee,' said Babbatunde, eventually. 'Cupcakes in the marquee. It's a special sort of big tent.'

'Grabbers well aware what is marshy, thank you,' said Granny Grabbers tartly.

28

Rehearsing

It had been a long afternoon.

They had practised some of the smaller tricks – including one where Granny Grabbers produced a rabbit out of her hat (except, of course, it was going to be a rather nervous gerbil).

This had gone badly on the first few attempts and Dr Doomy had ended up hanging by his front paws from Granny Grabbers' headlamp lashes.

However, by the third go it looked almost as if Granny Grabbers knew what she was doing.

She took the hat off, waved it about, reached inside and then Dr Doomy climbed helpfully on to the palm of her grabber and sat there while she showed him to the crowd.

'He's a lot smaller than a rabbit,' said Babbatunde, who was the only person present who had actually seen a real magic show.

'We'd ask a rabbit,' said Delilah. 'We just don't know any.'

In the end it was decided that perhaps Dr Doomy would be safer at home. Then all card tricks were abandoned after Granny Grabbers got a bit too enthusiastic when she was trying to shuffle the cards and punched herself in the headlamp by mistake.

After that they tried practising making animals out of balloons. According to the Rescue Plan, Delilah and Babbatunde would do this while Granny Grabbers moved the Vanishing Cupboard into the middle of the stage for the Grand Finale.

Delilah made a snake, which just looked like a balloon with eyes, and a cat, which looked like a camel.

'Make the animal first and then decide what it is afterwards,' suggested Babbatunde.

'So,' said Delilah, 'Is that a mouse eating a sausage?'

'It's not a mouse,' said Babbatunde. 'It's an African elephant.'

'Attention all child units,' said Granny Grabbers. 'Tidy up. Put away. Practice over.'

'But we can't do anything properly,' said Delilah desperately.

'And we haven't even got the special Vanishing Cupboard to practise *with*,' said Babbatunde.

Granny Grabbers waved anxiously at the window. Mr and Mrs Smart were outside getting loads of shopping out of the car. Home two hours earlier than normal.

The rehearsal was over.

29

Night Before the Party

That night Delilah and Babbatunde both slept badly. They were very worried. However, Granny Grabbers was by far the most worried of all. After an hour recharging her batteries in the utility room she trundled out into the moonlight.

Her headlamps faded from frightened purple to sorrowful blue and back to purple again. She had her photograph of Pug, and Sir Isaac's spare sunglasses in the pocket of her apron.

She stopped by the grabbmobile and looked at the photograph. Then she looked at the glasses. She sang some Dentists of Doom songs to try and keep her spirits up.

'Mouthy wash your worries away
If you haven't any tooth decay
It's OK
It's OK
Tomorrow is another minty new day . . .'

But Granny Grabbers didn't have any teeth and, for once, not even the Dentists could cheer her up.

She went into the garage and brought out the stepladder and lots of paint and brushes. Then, beeping sadly, she unfolded the ladder and bounced up the steps, swinging open cans of paint and brushes in her grabbers.

Hercules came over the wall. He had heard her voice. She threw him a piece of Mr Smart's new, improved fish muffin.

'Mouthy wash your worries away . . .' she sang in a shaky voice.

Perhaps Hercules was worrying too. Or

perhaps it was something to do with the new, improved fish muffin. Cats like fish a lot. They are not so keen on toffee. He tried to yowl but his back teeth were stuck together.

Granny Grabbers started painting with three brushes at once.

When the birds started singing and the sun came up the grabbmobile was scarlet and gold. So was the nearby grass and so, in places, was Hercules, who had made the mistake of dozing off under the ladder.

'Must not fail,' Granny Grabbers croaked to herself as she went slowly back to the house. 'Everybody depending on Grabbers.'

30

Leaving for the Party

It was lunchtime on the day of the party. Granny Grabbers was outside packing the magic tricks into the grabbmobile. Delilah and Babbatunde had just put on their grabber-made costumes.

Babbatunde's mother was in the living room with Mr and Mrs Smart having a cup of tea and very politely saying no thank you to scary muffins.

There had already been one dangerous moment when Mr Smart heard Granny Grabbers revving up the grabbmobile, which made him think about expensive motorbikes, which made him offer to take Sofia out for a blast on *his* expensive motorbike, which he thought was safe in the garage.

Fortunately Sofia had said no thank you, because she had just been the guest of honour at an air show and it had left her with a stiff neck. Then something else dangerous happened.

'I did not even know that Babbatunde had been invited to the birthday party for the Blingman twins,' she said.

'Well, we didn't know Delilah had been invited,' said Mr Smart. 'We had no idea at all.'

'Have you actually seen the invitation, Mr Smart?'

'Have we seen the invitation, darling?' Mr Smart asked Mrs Smart.

'DE-LI-LAH!' shouted Mrs Smart. 'Have we seen the invitation to the PAR-AR-TEE?'

She didn't need to shout. Delilah and Babbatunde were just outside the door, in the hall, having problems with their costumes.

'You're all lumpy,' whispered Babbatunde.

'It's the secret pockets. They're full of stuff . . .'

'DE-LI-LAAAAH!'

They looked at each other. They had, of course, no invitations to show anyone. All Delilah had said to her parents was that they were going to the party – which, alarmingly, was true.

Then, thank goodness, the doorbell rang.

Mr Smart came leaping out of the living room to answer it and stepped on Babbatunde's cloak, which was much too big and trailing along the floor.

There was a parcel delivery man at the front door.

'Special delivery, very heavy,' he said, pointing. 'Lady in the garden said OK to leave it down there by the, er, shed.'

'Lady?' said Mr Smart, peering outside.

'Lady with six arms and a big pointy hat,' said the man.

'Oh, that would be our childcare machine,' said Mr Smart. 'She can't talk, you know,' he added sternly. 'That's the more expensive model.'

The parcel delivery man looked puzzled. He had just had quite a long chat with Granny Grabbers about how to get paint off roses.

'Well, anyway, if someone would just sign here . . .'

'It's all right, Dad,' said Delilah quickly. 'It's something for the birthday party. We know all about it, don't we, Babbatunde? We'll go and unpack it.'

They hurried outside, leaving Mr Smart asking the innocent delivery man if he would like to try an experimental muffin.

There was a very big box squashing the grass next to the grabbmobile. Granny Grabbers was dithering around it, beeping.

'Too big for grabbmobile,' she muttered. 'Minty new day, minty new day. Everybody depend on Grabbers.'

She had scarlet and gold splodges all over her.

'Are you all right, Granny G?' asked Babbatunde. He placed a hand on one of her shoulders. She got a wheel tangled in his cloak.

'Let's ask Mr Adeleye if he will take it in the diplomatic car,' said Delilah. 'There's loads of room in there.'

Mr Adeleye had been firmly instructed by Sofia to take Delilah and Babbatunde to the party and to wait outside for them and take them home again.

'Goody idea, goody goody,' said Granny Grabbers, still sounding very worried. 'Grabbers must go oily the joints.'

She didn't really need to oil anything. She was still glugging a bit as it was.

Delilah and Babbatunde watched as she

went back into the house, presumably heading for her secret room.

'This is bad,' said Delilah.

The parcel delivery man hurried past them making choking noises.

'That's the sprout and marzipan flavour,' said Delilah sniffing. She put her hand in her sleeve to see if she had a paper hanky and pulled out something folded that immediately burst open and became a bunch of orange flowers and a cloud of pink sparkling smoke.

'I really wish we had more time to practise,' said Babbatunde when they'd both finished coughing. He took off his top hat and several real eggs fell out and broke on the path.

'So do I,' said Delilah.

'On the other hand,' said Babbatunde, trying to push bits of eggs into the flowerbed with his foot, 'Granny G has never been defeated yet.'

31

Madame Amazeyoo from Paris

They set off at last.

Granny Grabbers went ahead in the scarlet and gold grabbmobile with 'Madame Amazeyoo and her Amazing Magic Show' painted across the side. Babbatunde and Delilah and the very large box followed in the diplomatic car with Mr Adeleye.

'Rowdy bout nearly soon,' said his satnav. 'At rowdy bout go second left . . . no . . . Go thirdly, yes, thirdly left . . . apples are good for vitamins.'

'You said it, Granny G,' said Mr Adeleye.

Meanwhile, in the grabbmobile, Granny Grabbers was preparing herself for the mission. 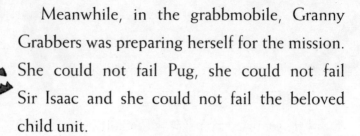 She could not fail Pug, she could not fail Sir Isaac and she could not fail the beloved child unit.

'No retreat and no suspender,' she said to herself.

Her headlamps flashed bright green with rage and bright red with excitement, confusing drivers coming from the other direction, who thought she must be some sort of moving traffic light.

'Do you have invitations?' asked the truly enormous security guard at the gate of the Blingmans' house.

'We are the children's entertainers,' said Babbatunde, straightening his spotted bow tie. 'This is our driver,' he added, pointing at Mr Adeleye, who was helping Delilah wrestle the big box out of the back of the diplomatic car.

Mr Adeleye, of course, was in his very smart chauffeur's uniform. The car was also impressive.

'I've just come from the Amanian Embassy,' said Babbatunde truthfully.

The security guard was consulting a list.

'Can't see you here,' he said. 'We've got Bouncy Castle with Bouncy Drawbridge, Miss Pompom and her Performing Poodles, The Paintball Pirates and . . . Cupcake Catering Company, Sickly Food for the Stars.'

'We were arranged at the last minute,' said Delilah. 'I see a lot of Dollie Blingman.' (This was true, if only on nosecam.) 'And, oh, you know, Godawfulla . . . um . . . Gobbledeplate.'

Babbatunde nudged her.

The grabbmobile was bumbling to a halt at the kerb. There was a wheelie bin stuck sideways on the front.

Babbatunde, Delilah and the enormous security man stared as the door at the back opened and a barrel-shaped person in silver and purple came out backwards, struggling to get her helmet off. It seemed to be jammed.

'Madame Amazeyoo,' said the security guard slowly, reading the writing on the side. 'And her Magic Show.'

'We do all the celebrity parties,' said Delilah desperately.

'Good afternoons, good afternoons,' said Granny Grabbers. She was wearing her six-armed magic coat, of course, three pairs of white gloves and a huge false moustache, which curled up at the sides. While the security guard continued to stare she managed to pull her helmet off, using all her grabbers at once. She stared back at him and lowered her headlamp lids with their very long lashes. Her headlamps turned a delicate shade of pink.

The security man had seen a few things in his time but he'd never seen anything quite like Madame Amazeyoo. He was speechless.

Delilah had just spotted Sir Isaac through

the gate. He was sitting on a table next to a pile of presents. He was wearing a blue and yellow dress.

Granny Grabbers held out a white-gloved grabber to the security guard and shook his hand very daintily.

'How doozy do,' she said in her husky voice. 'Delighty to meet you.'

The security man gazed into her headlamps. She fluttered her lids.

'We are from Paris,' said Granny Grabbers, sounding even more husky and mysterious.

The security guard opened the gate.

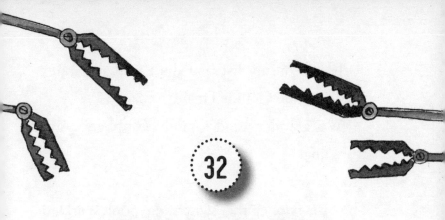

32

Events in the Tent

The garden was huge with a swimming pool, the bouncy castle and the marquee. There was a stage for the entertainment and a tent behind it with a sign saying 'Children's Entertainers Only'.

Granny Grabbers drove the grabbmobile and the security guard helped the others carry the large box and put it in the tent.

'When are you on?' he asked wistfully. 'Perhaps I'll get a chance to come and see your act.'

'Last,' said Granny Grabbers promptly.

'It said on my list that the Paintball Pirates are doing the Grande Finale.'

'We grander,' said Granny Grabbers. 'And more final.'

The sun shone, the swimming pool sparkled and the photographers arrived from *Yadda Yadda* magazine. Children in very expensive clothes wandered around eating cupcakes. The Blingman twins' birthday party had begun. The last chance to save Pug and Sir Isaac Newton before they were taken away to New York.

Delilah had seen Sir Isaac again on their way to the children's entertainers' tent. Dollie was carrying him as she walked along, with a group of girls bobbing around her.

'She's the most expensive bear in the world,' Dollie lied loudly. 'My dad paid ever so much money for her. She can talk. And she tried to electrify Billie because he was going to shave a skull and crossbones on her chest. I'm taking her to New York to show everyone at school. And I'm going to dye her fur pink all over.'

'O is for oh dear,' said a familiar mournful voice. 'H is for help.'

Delilah gritted her teeth and hurried after the others.

In their special tent the children's entertainers were preparing for their turns on the stage. Miss Pompom herself was calmly doing her make-up while her poodles did some gentle stretching and bending exercises.

The Paintball Pirates were cracking jokes and putting on their costumes and making sure their paintball guns were working.

Meanwhile, Madame Amazeyoo and her assistants fussed anxiously with their equipment. They had managed to get the big box open. It had turned out that, from the outside, the Vanishing Cupboard looked very like a wardrobe. Granny Grabbers unlocked it.

It looked very like a wardrobe inside too.

'There is space for a secret compartment at the back,' said Babbatunde, walking round it. 'And I can see some air holes. We just need the instructions on how to open it.'

They looked in the empty box. They looked around on the ground. They looked inside the cupboard again. There were no instructions.

'Having a problem, me hearties?' said the captain of the Paintball Pirates, who had just finished gluing on his beard.

'It's supposed to be a vanishing trick. Someone gets in the cupboard, we shut the door and open it again, and they've disappeared,' said Babbatunde. 'But we can't see how it works.'

'Ah, a secret compartment job,' said the captain. 'I've seen one of these before. Isn't there a button you press on the outside somewhere?' He began feeling round the edges of the cupboard. 'I like a bit of a puzzle. Here it is. I'll get in and you shut the door, and press this button here . . .' He showed Babbatunde the button hidden high up on the side of the cupboard near the back.

Then he stepped into the cupboard and closed the door without waiting for a reply. Everyone looked at the cupboard. Even the poodles.

No one spoke.

Granny Grabbers raised a grabber nervously to try and straighten the point on her hat. The poodles thought it was a command and all stood on their hind legs. She lowered her grabber. They sat down again.

Then she reached up as high as she could and just managed to press the button. There was a crunch and a rattling noise from inside the cupboard.

'Should we open it now?' whispered Delilah.

Beeping quietly, Granny Grabbers opened the cupboard again.

It had worked. The captain had vanished.

'Great!' said Babbatunde. 'What a relief. Let's close it again and get him back.'

Granny Grabbers closed the cupboard. She pressed the button. She waited a moment. Then she opened the cupboard again. Her headlamps turned purple with alarm.

The captain still wasn't there.

The other pirates, Madame Amazeyoo and her assistants, and Miss Pompom and her poodles all stared at the empty cupboard. 'Ssh!' hissed Delilah.

'Help!' called somebody somewhere in a very muffled voice. 'Get me out of here!'

There were some tapping noises, then thuds. Finally the whole cupboard began to rock. Just like the wardrobe had done at Blingman's when Pug had been trapped inside.

Immediately everyone was helping. The pirates pressed and then banged the button. The cupboard was tipped and shaken and sniffed (that was the poodles).

Then a security guard put his head in through the tent flap and said that it was time for Miss Pompom and her poodles to go on stage. She patted her hair and they followed her out in single file with the smallest one at the back.

Everyone else kept pressing the button. The button was stuck.

33

The Magicians Perform

It was still stuck twenty minutes later when Miss Pompom and her poodles came back.

'Very excitable crowd,' she said breathlessly. 'All that sugar. Noisy. I thought little Frou-frou here was going to fall off the tightrope because of all the shouting. But she made it, bless her.' (Yes, they were very talented poodles.)

Buzz Blingman came sideways in through the tent flap, chewing his worry beads.

'What's going on?' he asked anxiously when he saw everyone gathered round the cupboard. 'Where are the Paintball Pirates? The children are expecting them. In fact, they're getting very restless.'

'The captain's delayed,' said the pirate with the furry parrot stuck on his shoulder.

'And we can't go on without him,' added the pirate with the pigtail.

'Well, the magic act will have to go on now then,' said Buzz. 'My brother Vinnie is out there. He'll laugh for a week if things go wrong.'

Delilah peeked quickly out of the tent. A few of the guests were starting to throw cupcakes at each other. The atmosphere was not relaxed.

'Quick!' commanded Buzz. 'At once.'

Granny Grabbers, Babbatunde, Delilah and the two Paintball Pirates had no choice. Between them they carried the cupboard and the box of balloons out of the tent and up the steps on to the stage.

The terrible moment had come.

The two Paintball Pirates climbed back

down again, casting anxious glances back at the Vanishing Cupboard.

Buzz Blingman introduced Madame Amazeyoo and her Amazing Magic Show.

Silence fell. Cupcakes were no longer flying. All eyes were upon the three magicians – none of whom could do any magic at all.

Granny Grabbers approached the microphone, straightening her pointy hat and muttering. It sounded something like 'mouthy wash, mouthy wash . . .' which the audience thought must be some sort of spell.

She looked out at all the faces and smashed cupcakes. Mrs Blingman was sitting at the back with a lot of other important-looking mothers. Sir Isaac was on Dollie's knee at the front. Buzz Blingman and someone who looked like him but much more handsome was sitting next to him. This must be Vinnie, a guest at his niece and nephew's birthday party. He looked very pleased with himself.

The plan had been to choose Sir Isaac and Pug out of the audience, vanish them in the cupboard, create a diversion and then hide them in the grabbmobile and escape.

But the plan had gone wrong.

And where was Pug anyway?

There was a noise like someone emptying a box of marbles on to a tin roof. This was Granny Grabbers clearing her throat.

'Child units, addles and bear,' she said slowly. She was gesturing behind her back with several grabbers. Delilah and Babbatunde could see the gestures, which were meant for them. They just couldn't understand them.

'My two charmy assistants will make –' Granny Grabbers tried to remember a single balloon animal that had come out right '– a very rare animal . . . the six-legged giraffee with the horns. Nature for all.'

At this point the party guests were still listening to her. They had never seen a magician with six arms before.

Delilah and Babbatunde began blowing up balloons. Babbatunde accidentally burst the first balloon by blowing it up too much.

'That boy's got footprints on his coat,' said Dollie. (He had, of course: Mr Smart's footprints.) 'And it's much too big for him.'

'Balloons are for babies,' shouted the girl next to her, who had to be the famously lovable Godawfulla Gobblethwaite – she was holding a depressed-looking dog. 'These have to be the cheapest entertainers I've ever seen,' she added. 'I don't think they know how to do it.'

Granny Grabbers beeped into the microphone. She was calling Pug. She didn't need to. Here he came, being pushed and dragged by Billie Blingman, right through the middle of the guests, who started jumping out of the way. He was wearing a red scarf knotted round his head, he had a skull and crossbones drawn on his chest and he was

holding a paintball gun in every grabber – some
of them were upside down.

Delilah and Babbatunde had made a balloon
ostrich, possibly carrying a TV aerial in its beak.
Or a very big fork.

But nobody was looking at them any more.

'I've come to challenge the Paintball Pirates
to a duel,' shouted Billie. 'My robot against all
three of you.'

He had a hat crammed over his lack of curls,
a fake tattoo on his chin and yet another

paintball gun, which he was pointing up into the air. There was really no danger of him looking cute at all.

'Where are the pirates?' he shouted. 'They're supposed to be here NOW. They're supposed to be on after those silly dogs.'

Then he spotted Pigtail and Parrot, who had stayed at the side of the stage.

'Aha-ha! Robot, I command you to fire!'

Pug was swivelling his head from side to side, looking at everyone. He waved to a particularly small boy. The small boy waved back.

'Fire, robot!' yelled Billie.

Pug waved to Granny Grabbers. Then, with all eyes upon him, he dropped all the guns, extended a grabber and picked a daisy out of the grass. His headlamps turned red with happiness. He began to trundle towards the stage and Granny Grabbers with Billie hanging on to him trying to hold him back and failing completely.

One or two of the guests made the mistake of starting to laugh.

'We don't want anyone else shooting, that's not part of the act,' said Pigtail, no doubt trying to sound kind but firm. 'Please put your gun down and just enjoy the show.'

Billie let go of Pug, aimed his own gun at Pigtail and fired. He missed Pigtail. He hit the cupboard high up on the side.

The door swung open and there was the captain, blinking a bit.

'Yo-ho-ho!' he said hurriedly as soon as he saw the audience. He hadn't been able to hear much in the cupboard and was very surprised to find himself on the stage with fifty children looking at him. However, he was certainly a professional.

He took a deep breath, did a couple of brilliant backflips, which was how they always started the act, and then fired a paintball at Parrot.

He was a much better shot than Billie. Parrot dodged, which was also part of their act, did a handstand and fired back. All the pirates did backflips and somersaults in the air, firing as they went. They were really very good.

Unfortunately no one was watching them.

Billie Blingman was still firing all over the place. And six of the guests had seized the six guns that Pug had dropped. Paintballs were flying everywhere and in all directions. Mrs Blingman had already been splattered with blue, pink and green. In a matter of seconds Billie had hit a *Yadda Yadda* photographer, a pyramid of cupcakes and Vinnie Blingman.

Delilah and Babbatunde retreated behind

the Vanishing Cupboard, clutching the balloon ostrich and peering round it at the scene of battle. Anyone without a gun was throwing food. Anyone who couldn't find any food was throwing party bags. Vinnie Blingman shouted curses, trying to brush off the purple paint that was smeared all over his designer suit. Then he spotted Buzz, who was wading through the crowd towards Billie. Vinnie grinned. He snatched a gun off a nearby child and started firing it at his brother.

A green paintball exploded on Buzz Blingman's back. He turned round. Another hit him in the chest.

'Loser!' shouted Vinnie, grabbing another gun and waving them both in the air. 'Look around you, loser! Everything you do goes wrong!'

Billie saw Dollie and fired at her. Dollie held up Sir Isaac like a shield. The paintball hit a security man.

Delilah and Babbatunde threw down the ostrich and leapt off the stage.

But there was no need for them to rescue Sir Isaac. One person had remained calm throughout everything. That person was Granny Grabbers. She was beeping a message to Pug.

Pug threw a salute in her direction and trundled towards Dollie, ignoring the jelly, ice cream and paintballs splatting all over him. Dollie was throwing everything she could find at Billie. She had thrown both her shoes. As Pug approached she threw Sir Isaac. Pug caught him and threw him to Granny Grabbers. Sir Isaac sailed through the air, revolving slowly and thoughtfully, with his dress billowing and his glasses glinting in the sunshine. Granny Grabbers caught him very neatly, reached down from the stage and gave him to Delilah. Then Pug bounced up beside her and they started beeping happily together.

In the middle of all this drama and noise, Delilah hugged Sir Isaac Newton, while Babbatunde stood next to them, heroically shielding them with his own person and getting covered with food and paint in the process.

'E is for egg,' croaked Sir Isaac. And then he added in a much smaller voice that only she heard, 'D is for Delilah.'

But it wasn't over yet.

The riot was surging away across the garden. More ammunition was needed. Many guests ran off towards the marquee where there was still plenty of food left for throwing. Some urgently needed to get paint and jelly out of their hair and eyes: they jumped in the swimming pool and started splashing each other with blue, pink and purple water.

The captain of the Paintball Pirates shouted to Pigtail and Parrot and they scrambled down from the stage, pulling off beards and parrots as they went. (The pigtail was real.)

'Just get out of here, Mrs Amazing,' called the captain to Granny Grabbers. 'We'll all be getting the blame for this . . .'

He ducked as yet another paintball whizzed past. The rest of the garden was full of whooping and shouting and screaming. Here in front of the stage something serious was happening.

Vinnie and Buzz Blingman were locked in a terrible duel.

Vinnie still had two guns. He was laughing and leaping and shouting insults. Buzz had only one gun and no ammunition. But he wouldn't give in and he wouldn't run away. All he had left to fight with was a bag of sweets, which he was throwing in handfuls, as hard as he could. His worry beads were clenched between his teeth.

His face was pouring with sweat. He looked as desperate and determined as a real soldier in a real war.

'Let's go, Granny G,' said Delilah, tugging at Granny Grabbers' magic coat.

But Granny Grabbers was watching Vinnie Blingman. And her headlamps had turned lime green.

He didn't notice. Which was a shame for him. In fact, he chose that moment to jump on the stage and jeer down at Buzz, who was swaying on his feet after the latest direct paintball hit.

'I'm cleverer, I'm better-looking and I always win!' cried Vinnie. He paused for breath. He looked around him for something more to jeer about.

'Look at the pathetic acts you got for your kids' party! What's this? A talking dustbin on wheels? How much did you pay for that?'

In a single, multi-grabber movement, the

talking dustbin on wheels picked him up, shoved him in the cupboard and slammed it shut.

Buzz Blingman stood absolutely still with his mouth open.

No one spoke.

Granny Grabbers raised her pointy hat with a flourish and opened the cupboard. She had finally done a magic trick that worked. Vinnie Blingman had vanished.

'Madame Amazeyoo at your service,' she said to Buzz. 'We are grand and final.'

Buzz Blingman smiled. None of them had ever seen him smile before.

He stepped over upturned chairs and squashed party bags, jumped on to the stage and held out his hand to Granny Grabbers.

Muffled shouts came from inside the cupboard.

'Secret button to release,' said Granny Grabbers, glugging slightly. She pointed up at the button.

'Later, later . . .' said Buzz, at last able to speak. 'You're the Easter Bun, I mean Bunny, aren't you? I remember you from the store.'

The Vanishing Cupboard shook slightly. Buzz ignored it.

'You wanted to buy the prototype . . .' Buzz looked round at Pug, who waved a timid grabber. 'And Dollie insisted on having your bear . . .'

The cupboard shook a bit more violently.

'Seems to me,' said Buzz Blingman, still grinning, 'that Dollie and Billie can do without this robot and this bear.' He pointed into the distance towards the swimming pool. Dollie and Billie were rolling about on the grass, biting and kicking and pulling each other's ears.

'They get bored with things pretty quick,' said Buzz. 'I'd be glad to swap the robot and the bear for this cupboard, if you would consider it a deal.'

'Deal,' said Granny Grabbers at once. 'Big

much deal and bargains all round.'

'The trouble is,' continued Buzz, raising his eyebrows at Pug, 'this cupboard is likely to be a bit heavy, especially *now* . . . So, before you go, if the prototype could just carry it into the house, I'd be very much obliged. I seem to recall the prototype is very strong when it comes to lifting furniture.'

He was still grinning. He hadn't stopped.

So Pug picked up the Vanishing Cupboard and carried it over his head, and Madame Amazeyoo and her assistants followed through the battered remains of the garden, past the tilting marquee, the crowded swimming pool and the forlorn bouncy castle. Someone had punctured it somehow. It was hissing and getting smaller.

As they walked along, Buzz spoke into his mobile phone.

'Would you prepare my brother's private jet for take-off?' he said cheerfully. 'I want to use it to deliver a cupboard to New York as soon as possible.'

There was a question from the person on the other end.

'Just the cupboard,' said Buzz. 'Keep it upright. But don't open it, OK? That's important.'

34

Breakfast in the Garden

'Will you please explain again how and why we come to have this small extra childcare machine,' said Mr Smart sternly. He was about to eat his breakfast outside. Fortunately it was a warm, sunny morning. The kitchen chairs and table were on the patio and the grass, together with the rest of the Smarts' downstairs furniture and the double bed and the chest of drawers from the spare bedroom. (The wardrobe had not been touched. Pug didn't like playing with wardrobes.)

'He's – I mean *it's* – helping Granny Grabbers

with the spring cleaning,' said Delilah quickly. This was true. However, Granny Grabbers was only doing the spring cleaning in the first place because Pug had got bored in the night and started building things with furniture.

Here he was now, coming out of the house, beeping happy joy and greetings and wearing a daisy chain. Granny Grabbers followed, rattling and clucking with concentration.

She was carrying a tray of steaming mugs of

coffee; a freshly made pot of tea; bowls of cereal and a milk jug; a toast rack packed with hot toast; pots of butter, jam and marmalade; the morning paper and a delicious-looking pile of hot cross buns. Pug had been at the Smarts' house for three days and Granny Grabbers and Delilah had spent the whole time trying to distract Mr and Mrs Smart from all the things he was doing.

'I've just seen the new wallpaper in the living room,' said Mr Smart, tucking into a hot cross bun.

Delilah held her breath.

'It's so spacious in there now,' he added cheerfully. 'It's amazing what a difference it's made, having flowers instead of stripes. The room seems twice the size.'

Pug had decided to redecorate the room as a present for everybody. There was a good reason why it looked bigger – and it wasn't to do with the choice of wallpaper. He had papered the walls and then he had papered the grand piano, now hidden in the garage and awaiting medical attention.

'Darling, have you any idea why the washing machine is upside down?' asked Mrs Smart. 'Is it something to do with saving energy?'

Delilah frowned at this new surprise.

Fortunately Mr Smart wasn't listening. 'I must remember to make some special muffins for our dinner guests tonight. It is quite an honour to have the President and his beautiful wife and little Bobby Tondy coming over to celebrate our success in the Arm-Wrestling Competition at the Institute—'

'MY success,' said Mrs Smart. 'I won the Ladies' Section—'

'I would have won my section,' interrupted Mr Smart, whose arm was in a sling. 'That other man cheated.'

'He did not, darling,' said Mrs Smart, starting to laugh. 'He was just much stronger and better than you. That's why you went flying through the air like that . . .'

Delilah wandered off down the garden, planning to call Babbatunde on her mobile. However, something distracted her.

Hercules was outside the garage, pacing up and down, mewing and meowing, with his eyes wide, his ears back and his fur fluffed up.

'Are you all right?' asked Delilah. 'Do you want to go into the garage?'

Now that the grabbmobile had been dismantled, her father's expensive motorbike was safely back in there again. Together, of course, with the newly papered piano. Everything was supposed to be normal, including the shed.

Except she soon realized that things were not normal at all.

She went to open the garage doors. She yelled and jumped backwards.

The doors weren't there.

'Meow,' commented Hercules.

There was just wall where the doors should have been. Delilah patted the wall. Yes, it was a wall.

She walked slowly round the corner of the garage, feeling very weird. She went past the little window. The window she could see from her bedroom. The window that should be on the other side.

Then she came to the back of the garage, where it almost disappeared into the tangled, overgrown hedge. And there were the doors.

'The garage has been turned round,' she told Hercules, who knew that already. 'It's back to front.'

She turned round herself and started to walk slowly towards the house. As she came round the corner of the shrubbery she saw that Pug was dancing from wheel to wheel near the breakfast table holding the green wheelie bin and the black recycling bin over his head.

In full view of Mr and Mrs Smart, Pug began juggling with the bins.

Higher and higher they went while Pug, looking upwards, rolled closer and closer to the table.

'No!' cried Delilah.

Pug looked at her, just for an instant. But it was enough. He threw one of the bins too hard. It began to spin. Then it turned upside down in the air.

Mr and Mrs Smart were showered with mouldy orange peel, rotting bananas, blobs of fat and slimy, uncooked experimental muffin mixture. Then the upturned bin landed very exactly on top of Mr Smart and he disappeared completely.

After a moment, he lifted the bin off himself in a slow and thoughtful manner. It was hard to see his face because of all the rubbish but he definitely did not seem relaxed.

'You look like something that's crawled out

of a drain!' screamed Mrs Smart, laughing tremendously and unable, at this stage, to see herself.

Granny Grabbers came hurtling out of the house, tangled in her apron and beeping at full volume, and began dabbing at Mr and Mrs Smart with a tea towel.

Pug buried his headlamps in his grabbers for a moment, then, as Delilah went to try and comfort him, he backed into a flowerbed, knocked over a chair and shot indoors.

'I am going to get the hose out of the garage,' said Mr Smart, sounding very, very cross. 'And I am going to wash this entire patio, and the table, and the chairs . . .'

Delilah was powerless. She watched in horror as he stalked off to the garage.

There was a short silence.

'Have we lent the garage doors to anyone, darling?' shouted Mr Smart. 'I don't seem to be able to find them.'

35

Under the Bed

'Please come out, Pug,' said Delilah, standing next to her bed. 'Granny Grabbers isn't angry. I'm not angry. We're just worried, that's all . . . We need to find somewhere for you to live where you can, well, express yourself.'

The bed wasn't standing on the floor. It seemed to be floating and it kept bobbing about. This was because Pug was hiding underneath. The bed was balanced on his head.

Sir Isaac, who usually had his afternoon nap there, was sitting on the pillow wearing a daisy chain (probably not something he would have

chosen, but Pug loved giving presents). He was also wearing the sort of hard hat people wear for protection on dangerous building sites. Although she had no way of telling, Delilah had the feeling that he was somewhat tense.

The bed lurched. Sir Isaac's glasses fell off.

Delilah crouched and lifted the cover, which was hanging down like a curtain. A pair of headlamps shone out at her. Dark, sorrowful blue.

'Granny Grabbers and I are going to keep thinking, and . . .' she tried to sound positive, 'thinking . . . and we won't stop until we've got a plan.'

There was a tiny beeping noise. Delilah was determined to learn Morse code, but she hadn't managed it yet. She squeezed Sir Isaac's paws and put his glasses back on. Then, with a promise to come back soon, she set off downstairs.

The awful truth was that Mr Smart had telephoned Happy Home Robotics as soon as he had finished telling the police that his garage doors had been stolen. Happy Home Robotics were coming to fetch Pug in the morning.

Granny Grabbers was sitting at her laptop looking at their website now.

'We many lorries all over country,' she intoned, reading from the bit called Robot Retrieval. 'We pick up problem robot in twenty-four hours.'

Delilah stared miserably at

the screen. There was a picture of a shiny, clean lorry and its shiny, clean driver.

'I bet Pug could pick the *lorry* up,' she said.

Granny Grabbers froze. Then she started whirring and buzzing. Her eyes flashed scarlet. She was having an idea.

'Boy Genie and esteemed parents visit dinner tonight?'

'Yes,' said Delilah. 'But how—'

Granny Grabbers engulfed Delilah in a six-grabber hug.

'Breaking news,' she said. 'Child units and Grabbers must be cunning and stealthy like the fox. Nature for all.'

36

Party at the Smarts'

'Are you sure that you are all right, Granny G?' asked Mr Adeleye. 'You must not be anxious, you know. Everything is going to be fine.'

Granny Grabbers was fidgeting round the kitchen. She had already done the washing-up and cleared away the plate that she had broken. Now she was trying to make after-dinner coffee for the guests. Sounds of merriment and voices came down the hall from the living room. The danger of being offered more deep-fried baked bean muffin was over, and the President and Sofia were giggling with relief.

'Skullduggerment is about to start,' said Granny Grabbers to Mr Adeleye. 'Grabbers much thanks esteemed friend.'

'I'm happy to help you, Granny G,' said Mr Adeleye. And he put a comforting hand on one of her shoulders.

'Do not worry about me,' said Mr Adeleye. 'You make all the skullduggerment you need.'

Outside in the garden, Delilah and Babbatunde were huddled behind the shed.

'Are you sure that you are all right, Delilah?' whispered Babbatunde.

'It's just that if this doesn't work,' said Delilah quietly, 'there's no time to organize anything else. And the man at Happy Home Robotics told my dad on the phone that they would absolutely never let Pug out of the laboratory again this time. It's because he caused them so much bad publicity on live TV when he got in a muddle on the roof of Blingman's, with the stupid Sort-It Squad.'

'Granny Grabbers' ideas always work,' said Babbatunde firmly.

Delilah sniffed.

'In the end,' he added.

They both looked up at the lighted windows of the house. Then they crept away out of the shadow of the shed. Not towards the house, however. They were going towards the long, dark shape of the diplomatic car, parked outside on the road. Babbatunde pulled something out of his pocket. It was the key to the boot.

Meanwhile, in the house, the guests were putting on their coats. A few moments later Delilah and Babbatunde were back indoors and Delilah was tiptoeing upstairs to fetch Sir Isaac.

'You look very nice with your daisy chain,' said Delilah. 'You should wear one more often.'

'N is for negative, not and no way,' said Sir Isaac, tersely.

*　*　*

Downstairs in the kitchen, Mr Adeleye finished his piece of delicious grabber-made chocolate cake. Then he went into the utility room, where Pug and Granny Grabbers were beeping softly together in Morse code.

'All the systems are go,' Granny Grabbers informed him.

He nodded, winked at Pug and went out into the garden.

Mr and Mrs Smart were coming out of the front door, both talking at once. The President was with them, of course, but he was listening. He was very good at it.

Mr Adeleye strode down the path. By the time they reached the car he was already standing beside it with the boot open and a solemn look on his face.

'I regret to inform you that we have a flat tyre,' he announced.

The front tyre, nearest to the pavement, was indeed most definitely flat. It looked as if almost every molecule of air had been let out of it. Which they had been.

The President smiled.

'But it is a small matter to change the tyre,' he said. 'I will help you, Mr Adeleye.'

'I am sorry but we do not have the jack to raise the car. It is not in the boot,' said Mr Adeleye.

'No problem, you can borrow ours,' said Mr Smart, full of enthusiasm. 'Oh no, you can't,' he added immediately. 'Ours is in the garage and we can't open the garage doors because they've been stolen.'

The President, Sofia and Mr Adeleye stared at him.

Delilah nudged Babbatunde.

'Dad,' said Babbatunde, 'let's ask the small childcare robot. He, I mean it, can lift anything. It's incredibly strong.'

'Absolutely not,' said Mr Smart. 'That machine is locked in the utility room until tomorrow, when it goes back to the manufacturer's. It is a menace to society. It spilt rubbish all over my hair.'

'Is it just like Granny G but smaller?' Sofia asked Delilah.

'Yes,' said Delilah. 'Much smaller.'

As if they had been waiting behind some bushes for the right moment (which they had) Granny Grabbers and Pug came trundling down the path and out of the gate.

'Oh, he's so cute!' cried Sofia. 'Look at his cute little grabbers and his cute little headlamps!' She patted Pug on the top of his head.

Delilah grinned and hugged Sir Isaac.

'Y is for yuck,' he muttered.

'Granny Grabbers,' said Delilah quickly, 'Mr Adeleye's car has a flat tyre.'

Pug rolled forwards, picked up the front of the car and stood underneath it, holding it above his head.

'S is for show-off,' growled Sir Isaac.

Mr Adeleye changed the tyre extremely quickly and efficiently. Then Pug put the car back down on the road and saluted.

Granny Grabbers beeped something very fast at low volume. Pug beeped back. The President looked at them both with a thoughtful expression.

'Pug could pick up the car and turn it right round completely in a cramped situation. Or he could pull it out of mud,' said Babbatunde.

'And if your car broke down he could carry it home,' added Delilah.

'With all of us in it,' said Babbatunde.

'Well, I think it's a brilliant idea,' said Sofia. 'He must come and live with us. We have several big cars, and they do break down sometimes. And I'm sure if Mr Pug has plenty to do he will not get into any of this trouble with throwing rubbish, Mr Smart.'

Pug beeped. Granny Grabbers replied.

The President was standing closest to the

garden wall. Perhaps he had already noticed that Mr Adeleye's jack for lifting up the car had mysteriously found its way out of the boot and under the roses in the Smarts' garden. Or maybe there was some other reason why he looked at Granny Grabbers and raised his eyebrows.

He cleared his throat. Everyone fell silent.

Granny Grabbers' eyes were purple with worry. She extended a rattling grabber and put it round Pug.

'I think this is a splendid idea, don't you agree, Mr Adeleye?' said the President.

'Yes, I do,' said Mr Adeleye.

Mr and Mrs Smart both gasped and started

talking loudly about how dangerous Pug was, while Sofia nodded and ignored them and patted Pug on the head again.

'And I am very interested to know that someone let down the tyre on my car on purpose so that Mr Pug would have a chance to show us all how useful he can be,' whispered the President. 'And that Granny G is pleased that her plan has worked because Mr Pug will be safe now because I am wise and kind and have a big garden, a helicopter and no, how do you say . . . *tip bang* stairs.'

Delilah and Babbatunde stared at him in amazement.

'I was in the Air Force when I was younger,' explained the President. 'We learnt Morse code.'

* * *

Acknowledgements

Many thanks to –

Elaine Mechergui and the staff at the Ferns, whose dedication to their work gave me the peace of mind to finish this book. *Nil satis nisi optimum*.

At AP Watt: Caradoc King, literary agent and Voice of the Bear; Louise Lamont, Elinor Cooper and, in the early history of Grabbers, Judith Evans.

At Hodder Children's Books: Beverley Birch (who commissioned Granny G), Naomi Pottesman (hard-working and forbearing editor), Chris Fraser, Rebecca Hearne, Andrew Nolan and everyone else behind the scenes, who has been and is still involved.

Hazel Cotton and Sarah Taylor-Fergusson.

Pete Williamson, who has once again captured Granny Grabbers brilliantly in his artwork.

J Salieri for editorial comment, early sketches, design ideas, patience and tech support.

Anna Bendinck, very talented voice artist, and W F Howes Ltd, audio books.

The writer Sandra Horn, for her early editorial comments and Bettina Vettori, who also knew Granny G from the beginning.

Steve and Diana Kimpton, web designers at The Word Pool.

Chris and Clara Sanders for technical advice and design feedback.

Caroline and Lindsay Rose for advice on social media options.

Catherine Fortune, especially for her help on 4 October 2012.

David and Mary Jackson who have given their valued long distant support over many years.

Trevor and Rosemary Whitbread who have been, as ever, generous and helpful.

And last but not least, Everyone on the Sunnyside of the Street.

GRANNY GRABBERS

Delilah Smart's life hasn't been the same since childcare robot Granny Grabbers entered her world and made it whizz bang wonderful fun. And it's not long before Granny Grabbers and Delilah stumble upon their next adventure...

'Hilarious'
Parents in Touch

'The perfect amount of mischief and mayhem'
The Golden Treasury Review